BOB AND THE BLACK KNIGHT

by Joseph Caldara

Bob and the Black Knight

ISBN 10: 0-9984298-4-8
ISBN 13: 978-0-9984298-4-7

Edited by Joseph Caldara and Cathy O'Brien-Humphreys
www.bobandthecyberllama.com

Printed in the United States of America

TABLE OF CONTENTS

Chapter 1

Jeeves tapped his hoof and raised his leg, looking at the watch he wasn't wearing. "Are you quite ready yet, sir?"

"Almost."

"Well, be quick about it. I'd like to leave for England before last night's dinner passes into my fourth stomach compartment.

"I didn't need to know that. Anyway, I'm just finishing up a few last-minute preparations."

"Sir, the doctor said that cream only needs to be applied every five hours and—"

"Not those preparations!"

Stumbling a bit, Bob stepped out of the front door, his Hawaiian shirt concealing his slight paunch. His brown hair was slightly askew and he wore a small, canvas backpack. On his side was a sizeable laser pistol, and he held a heater shield, which featured a crest of crossed rubber chickens.

"The Halibut Coat of Arms," Jeeves remarked, raising his eyebrows, "Excellent choice,, sir. But why the backpack?"

"I want to be more prepared this time. I'm tired of having to rely on your cybernetic implants to get me out of danger."

Jeeves snorted, crinkling his llama nose and adjusting his monocle. "Edwina never brought a sack full of supplies to an adventure, sir."

"Well, I'm not my grandmother. You should give me a break. I'm still new to the whole treasure-hunting adventurer thing."

"Nobody benefits from low expectations, sir," Jeeves grumbled.

Bob heard the gears inside his cybernetic llama whir and click as Jeeves turned his head. His eyes narrowed as he stared at his employer's side.

"No longsword, sir?"

"What? No."

"But we're going to England in search of a priceless, medieval artifact. I thought you might—"

"Bring a sword to a gunfight? No thanks."

"You are a pragmatic soul, sir, there's no doubt. And I mean that in the most demeaning way possible. Now, hop on. I've used the atmospheric sensors in my armpit fur to measure the air currents. If we leave now, we'll make excellent time."

As soon as his master had clambered onto his back (and left a few unsightly scuff marks on his suit jacket), Jeeves activated his rectum rocket, and the two blasted off.

Kicking up a cloud of dust, the flying cyber-llama expertly touched down in Cornwall just outside Altarnun. Jeeves took a deep breath and sighed.

"Here we are, sir. One of the world's great historical sites. Anything you'd like to see before we begin the adventure?"

"A trash can," Bob moaned, grasping his belly.

Jeeves rolled his eyes. "You have the stomach of an octogenarian and the courage of a sea cucumber. We best examine

3

the scabbard before entering the city. You should never whip out your ancient artifacts in a crowded area."

Bob loosened the ties on his puke-green backpack and uncovered the ancient sheath. Though he'd seen it before, he was still taken aback. The black metal bore the basic shape of a sword, but was covered in carvings and etchings, some readable and others worn away by age. Sunlight glistened off the gems that coated the scabbard and almost blinded the young adventurer. The rubies, sapphires, emeralds, diamonds, and innumerable other stones glowed like fireflies.

Jeeves nodded. "There's no doubt about it. The gems have started glowing again. The scabbard knows its blade has fallen into the wrong hands. We'll need to begin our hunt for Excalibur immediately, sir."

"Okay. Uh...where do we start?"

Jeeves' metal, tentacle-like arm snaked out of his back, and he stroked his furry chin. His head jutted downward and snapped onto the scabbard. Then he began sniffing the sheath like a bloodhound.

"Are you…feeling okay, Jeeves?"

The llama took one last, long sniff and poked his head up. "Indeed, sir. I've uncovered our first lead. There's no mistaking it: my nasal analytic systems have detected the Lady's B.O."

"The what?"

"Her body odor, sir. The stench produced by accumulated, aged sweat."

"No, I know what B.O. is. Why does the scabbard smell like a woman's B.O.? And why does it matter?"

"Not just any woman, sir. The Lady of the Lake," Jeeves said, sniffing the air and trotting toward the city, "The mysterious, magical mistress of Arthurian lore. Edwina had my half-mechanized brain programmed with the distinctive fragrance of her armpit sweat."

"Why?"

"You never know when that kind of knowledge might come in handy, sir. I also know what Genghis Kahn and Augustus Caesar smelled like. And I'll have you know, sir, that the first Roman emperor was rather ripe."

5

Bob jogged alongside Jeeves, trying to match the llama's pace. "So we're trying to find the Lady of the Lake?"

"Yes. Did you read up on the King Arthur legends before we left?"

"No."

"I thought not," Jeeves sighed, "According to legend, the Lady of the Lake was the keeper of Excalibur. Early in his career, King Arthur had an encounter with a particularly-nasty knight clad in jet-black armor. They battled for hours, but at last, a mighty blow from the Black Knight shattered the king's sword like an ostrich egg. Before the knight could slay him, the wizard Merlin transported Arthur to a mystical lake in search of a new, more-kingly sword.

"In the middle of the lake was a woman's hand grasping a bejeweled sword. Merlin explained to Arthur that that only the most noble of knights could take the ancient blade from that hand before it disappeared beneath the lake. Arthur sailed to the middle of the lake and, being King Arthur and all, had no trouble taking the sword.

6

"After he returned to shore, a beautiful maiden emerged from the middle of the lake, walked to shore, and introduced herself as the Lady of the Lake.

"The mysterious woman told the king that she would lend him the sword on one condition: that he return it before his death. True to his word, Arthur managed to toss both Excalibur and its scabbard back into the lake just before he breathed his last."

"And we're going to find out if the Lady of the Lake is real?" Bob asked.

"Oh, she's real alright. And a terrible poker player. How do you think your grandmother wound up with the scabbard?"

It took hours to traverse the sparse farms and villages of Altarnun, and Bob and Jeeves got more than a few awkward stares. Every few moments, Jeeves would jut his head in the air, inhale, and trot in a new direction. Eventually, the two stood before a forested area outside the city limits. The sounds of the parishes faded away, replaced by the chirping of birds and the chittering of squirrels.

"I'm not sure about this forest, Jeeves," Bob said, glancing over his shoulder at a suspicious shadow.

"Of course you aren't, sir. There's a reason they call it a magic forest."

"Wow. So we might encounter some elves or pixies or something?"

Jeeves shot his master a disappointed look. "This is reality, sir, not some fantasy novel. If I were you, I'd stay focused on the creatures that actually exist. Watch out for the gnomes, though. They'll slice your tendons."

Bob kept walking, glancing nervously at his heels every few seconds. The rustling sounds coming from the grass weren't relaxing anymore.

After a few anxiety-ridden minutes, he bumped into Jeeves' furry behind. The llama had stopped. Before them was an enormous lake, blue and shimmering. It sat in the middle of a clearing, and the sun, no longer hidden by the trees' shadows, warmed Bob's skin. The water was motionless, and no animals or fish could be seen.

Jeeves inhaled. "This is the place, sir. I'm sure of it."

"Alright," Bob said, looking at his heels one more time just to be sure. "But where's the Lady?"

"Summoning the Lady of the Lake has always been something of a shot in the dark," Jeeves replied, "Perhaps we should try using the scabbard."

Bob nodded and pulled the ancient sheath from his backpack. Kneeling Bob rapped the surface of the lake with the end of the scabbard. A large ripple made its way across the lake, and Bob heard a faint ringing.

Stillness returned to the lake. As he watched the surface of the water intently, Bob noticed a small patch of black hair creeping toward him. The patch turned into a head, then shoulders, and soon Bob and his llama beheld a woman clad in white sauntering toward them.

Her waist-long hair and light skin were completely dry, and her intricate gown sparkled in the sun, though it didn't hurt Bob's eyes at all. The lady was gorgeous, and Bob blushed a little as she looked in his direction.

"Greetings, noble sirs," she said in a wistful voice, "Thou hast summoned me from this ancient lake using the scabbard of the sword Excalibur. To what end, may I ask?"

"Good day, madam," said Jeeves, "This is Bob Halibut, son of Filbert Halibut, son of Edwina Halibut. You gave her the scabbard of Excalibur many years ago."

"Many souls have I met over the centuries, steed."

"Of course. A thousand pardons, good lady. We come to your lake because the scabbard's gems have begun glowing. We know the sword has been lost and were hoping you could aid us in our quest to retrieve it."

The Lady took a step back, furling her eyebrows. "The blade is not lost," she said, "I hath kept it secure all these years. If thou art truly a friend, I will show it to thee."

"Yes. Thank you," Bob stammered.

Whirling on her heels, the Lady strode back into the lake. She emerged a few minutes later cradling a curious object. As the Lady drew closer, Bob realized that she was holding a toilet

10

plunger. Her hand gripped the end of the wooden handle as if it were a sword hilt, and the rubber cup rested on her palm as if it were a blade.

"Behold the sword Excalibur!" she proclaimed.

"Uh...that's a toilet plunger," Bob said.

"Thou art mistaken, weary traveler," the Lady said, swinging the toilet plunger through the air, "'Tis Excalibur, the bane of all evil and savior of the good."

"No, I'm afraid my young companion is correct," said Jeeves, "That's nothing more than a bathroom appliance."

"Then I shall return with the mystic blade. Await my return here." The Lady dropped the toilet plunger and sauntered back into the lake. She broke the surface of the water once again, this time carrying an oversized, orange, foam hand with the index finger outstretched and "We're #1" printed on the front.

"Behold the sword Excalibur!" she shouted once again.

"No, it isn't," Bob said, shifting uncomfortably, "It's just a foam finger."

The Lady stared at Bob sternly. "Thou must prove thyself worthy if thou wishest to wield this blade, young warrior," she said, ignoring his last comment, "for with it comes great and terrible power."

"My young master cannot slay evil with sports memorabilia, madam," Jeeves piped up, "Does not a sword need a hilt and a blade?"

The Lady glanced from the foam finger to Bob and then back to the finger. She dropped it to the ground and turned to the lake once again, disappearing beneath the water.

"What's going on?" Bob asked.

"I'm afraid the centuries have taken their toll on the Lady," Jeeves said, shaking his head, "She may not look it, but she's lived many, many years. Dementia catches up with many people eventually, even creatures of myth."

Bob's heart sank. "Should we just leave, then?"

"Yes, I think that'd be best, sir," Jeeves said.

"Behold the sword Excalibur!" the Lady shouted as she held aloft five tickets to "Frankenstein on Ice."

The forest dimmed as evening set in. Staring at the forest floor, Bob sighed and trudged back toward Altarnun. Jeeves trotted just behind him, his fluffy bottom bouncing as usual.

"Well, sir, where to now?"

"Huh? Oh, I thought we'd just head back to town. Maybe we can find a historian who knows where the sword might be."

"What? Sir, I'd have thought you'd learned your lesson by now about trusting strangers with adventuring details."

"Well, I don't see what else we can do. We flew across the Atlantic to watch some woman walk out of a pond and swing a toilet plunger around."

Jeeves snorted. "A day of exploring a magic forest would yield much better results than a talk with some stuffy historian. And, if I may be so bold, it'd be a great deal more fun."

"I don't have a say in this, do I?"

"No, you don't. Now come, sir, that path through the trees looks promising."

The golden light of the sun turned to gray and then to black as Bob and Jeeves followed the lone path. Thin gusts of fog began to roll in, and Bob shivered, glancing enviously at Jeeves' fur. The llama scanned every part of the forest, reading every tree, flower, and blade of grass with his sensors. At last, he stopped.

"This looks like as good a spot as any to make camp. A well-rested adventurer is a happy adventurer and I dare say I'm in need of a recharge."

Bob nodded and opened his backpack. "I brought a sleeping bag. The ground looks pretty flat over—"

Jeeves scoffed. "Sleeping bag," he chuckled, "I hope you didn't think I was without sleeping accommodations, sir." Raising a hoof to his nose, Jeeves covered his left nostril and blew out his right. Like a giant wad of slimy tissue, a dark green sleeping bag shot from the llama's nose and hit the ground, unfurling.

"You'd best get in while it's still nice and moist," he said, "Goodnight, sir."

"Halibut…"

Bob's eyes popped open. The nostril-holstered bedroll was actually pretty comfortable, and Bob had been sleeping like a raccoon on horse tranquilizers. The fog was thicker now; it hid most of the ground like a cloud of ghostly mashed potatoes. Jeeves stood A few feet away, motionless.

Bob leaned back once again. Just as his eyelids drooped shut, he heard the sound he had before:

"Halibut..."

It was a moaning voice, wailing but authoritative. Bob sat up and reached for his laser pistol. His fingers curled around the cold steel grip, and he drew the pistol, swallowing. The darkness and fog had made most of the forest invisible.

Bob focused on the trees, thinking at every moment he saw something darting between them. The sturdy plants appeared to be nothing more than motionless black shapes silhouetted against the mists and bushes. And then one of them moved.

"The castle, Halibut...the answers you seek..."

As the shape came into view, Bob made out arms, legs, and a head, all completely covered in armor. The figure held a heater

15

shield, the same shape as Bob's, which bore no device or symbol. In its other hand was a longsword as long as Peter Dinklage was tall. Droplets of mist clung to the sword, and the moonlight shimmered off the blade.

His hands quaking, Bob couldn't bring himself to fire the laser pistol. Blinking the sweat out of his eyes, he began to see the figure more clearly. The knight's helmet was a long cylinder, flat on top with two eye slits. Like the shield, neither his shin plates, breastplate, shoulder-armor, gauntlets, greaves, or back plate bore any markings.

Even in the darkness, Bob could tell that the armor was black. Jet black. Blacker than a cougar rolling around in coal soot and tar at midnight.

The black knight drew closer, almost floating, and stopped inches in front of Bob. The young adventurer glanced nervously at Jeeves, but the motionless llama was no help.

"Halibut," the knight said, more firmly this time, "My castle…the answers you seek…in the heart of the castle…"

16

With a swish of mist, the black knight vanished. Panting, Bob dropped to his knees, mouth open wide. Jeeves' eyes slid open, his spectral sensors activated, and he sauntered to his master's side.

"Are you quite alright, sir?" he asked, "You look as if you've seen a ghost."

Chapter 2

"It said what, sir?"

"The castle. The ghost said we can find the answers we seek inside its castle."

"Well, at least we have some clue to go on now. Your family always did have a way of attracting crackpot supernatural beings. Did this apparition happen to mention how we might go about finding this castle?"

"No. The whole thing was pretty vague and mysterious."

Jeeves shook his head and sighed. "Spectral gentlemen tend to be like that, I'm afraid. Always speaking in prophecies and riddles and the like. I remember when the ghost of Henry the Fifth haunted Edwina's attic for a week. It took us days to figure out that by warning us that 'the grating of the steel parchment echoes

18

throughout the crevice' he was trying say we needed to buy higher-quality toilet paper."

Bob couldn't tell whether or not they were making progress. The trees, bushes, and other shrubbery blended together and he found himself daydreaming and dozing on his feet as he trudged along. A yell from the llama yanked Bob out of his trance:

"Look there, sir! The three maidens!"

Jeeves pointed to a square, wooden structure. It was hard to make out, but Bob could see three figures moving around behind it. "The what?"

"The three maidens. You'd no doubt know about the maidens if you'd read up on Arthurian myths, as you were instructed, but according to the Excalibur legend, King Arthur located the Black Knight's castle with the help of three mystical maidens he met in the forest. And they're just ahead!"

Bob jogged alongside his llama, grinning. A lead at last! As they neared the structure, three maidens did indeed come into view. All three wore long, flowing dresses and had daisies, pansies, and other flowers braided into their shiny hair. Each one sat in a folding chair behind a wooden stand labeled "Information and Vacation Packages."

"Good morrow to you, fair ladies," Jeeves said, making a cap-tipping motion with his mechanical arm, "We are travelers, noble warriors from across the great sea, who seek adventure and noble quests. We have heard tell that thou knowest the way to the castle of the Black Knight. I implore you, please, provide us with such guidance."

One of the maidens sighed and raised a nail file to her fingernails. "Yeah," she said, staring at her nails and thrusting a pamphlet into Bob's hands, "Just follow the map."

The young adventurer unfurled the colorful pamphlet titled "The Mystic Forest: a Peaceful Holiday Getaway." Flipping through pages of ads for local attractions and hotels and a series of restaurant coupons, he at last found a cartoon image of a stone structure labeled "Black Knight's Castle." A convenient map pictured a short path leading straight to the castle gate.

Another of the maidens removed her headset. "Would you be interested in our Black Knight vacation package, sir?" she said,

20

snapping her gum, "It includes a tour of the Pixie's Toadstools and the Meadow of Sorrows, as well as a discounted rate on your hotel room."

"Go for the upsell, Sheila," the third young woman whispered.

"Oh, yeah. And for an extra forty pounds, we can upgrade you to Platinum Status, which includes a pre-tour breakfast and a souvenir jar of sleeping potion."

"Thank you, good woman," Jeeves said, "Your offer of Platinum Status does my heart good, but methinks my young companion and I must ride on, continuing our noble quest."

"Whatever," the first maiden said, blowing on her fingernails, "Thank you for choosing the Mystic Forest. Have a magical day."

The foliage thinned, and the sunlight streamed onto the stone bridge before them. Though the bridge was sturdy, the stones were covered in moss and ivy and were cracked with age. Beyond the bridge was a grass-covered hill, beyond which loomed the castle they sought.

Jeeves clip-clopped across the bridge while Bob kept his eyes out for trolls. Across the bridge now, Bob scanned the castle and scratched his head. The square keep was sealed up tight, the stones fit so closely together they looked like corn kernels on a cob. Inside the outer wall was a single tower that overshadowed the rest of the landscape like a Saint Bernard among Yorkies.

The front lawn was coated in golf course-green grass, but contained only a single tree, an apple tree that bore no fruit. Instead, the tree was covered in rusted shields. Heater shields, bucklers, kite shields, parmas, and tower shields hung from the branches. Rust and dust obscured the shield's crests, but it was clear that many knights had traveled to this castle.

Resting against the base of the tree was another shield, a black one with no design. A black battle hammer, overgrown with weeds, lay before the shield.

Jeeves cleared his throat. "Sir, I'm not sure your ethereal friend knows we're here. Perhaps you should 'ring the doorbell,' as it were."

Bob nodded and hefted the hammer, scattering dirt and grass. Struggling to keep the weapon balanced, he aimed at the shield and swung. The hammer head slammed into the shield, and Bob felt vibrations ripple through his arms. A gong-like banging echoed throughout the forest, followed by an unbroken ringing.

Then there was silence. Bob heard a series of clicks, sliding metal, and shifting gears. The castle gate groaned open and fell to the dirt with a thud. Hooves cracking, a black steed, complete with black saddle and black reigns, thundered out of the castle. Atop the horse was the figure Bob had seen last night. Though he'd seen the Black Knight before, Bob swallowed hard.

The sable warrior hopped off his horse and strode toward Bob. He carried two wooden lances, long and painful-looking, and without saying a word, handed one to the young adventurer.

Bob accepted the lance. Trying not to let his knees shake, he cleared his throat. "Um…*ahem*…hello, good sir. Uh…what are the lances for?"

"Inside my fortress do indeed lie the answers you seek, young warrior," the Black Knight answered in a booming voice, "But not all may quest for the sword Excalibur. Thou must prove thyself a noble soul and a worthy opponent if thou wishest for my guidance. Let us begin with the second requirement."

The ancient knight mounted his horse and galloped back toward the castle. As soon as it reached the gate, the black steed whirled around, and the warrior pointed his lance straight at Bob's head.

"What's going on?" Bob asked Jeeves, already knowing and dreading the answer.

"The Black Knight will only deal with those who prove themselves in battle, sir." Jeeves knelt. "Now hop on and grab your shield. I'm sorry there wasn't time for a jousting lesson before we left, but you'll just have to learn as we go."

"What?! But Jeeves, I—"

"Steady the lance, sir."

"Okay, but you're going to shoot him with some sort of mechanical gadget at the last minute, right? You'll hit him with the nacho cheese cannon or something?"

"I'm afraid not, sir. Knights, samurai, and their ilk are sticklers for honor codes. If you use anything but what you have on your person to fight the Black Knight, he may not lead us to Excalibur."

"But—"

"Steady the lance, sir."

Bob hopped on Jeeves' back, and the llama stood, Bob's lance wobbling like a see-saw. Just as he began to get the hang of balancing the lance, Jeeves lurched forward, galloping at a pace Bob hadn't seen since their trip to Mexico.

The Black Knight's horse charged, snorting. The armored warrior leaned forward, reducing wind resistance, and held his shield in front of his heart. Judging by his opponent's unarmored potbelly, the joust would be over quickly.

A blast of wind hit Bob as his llama companion picked up speed, making a beeline for the Black Knight. The clopping of both Jeeves' and the horse's hooves sounded like a hundred base drums. Bob blinked the dust and tears from his eyes and squinted, trying to study the knight barreling toward him. All he could think to do was to copy the Black Knight's stance, crouching and preparing to meet the phantom's lance with his shield.

Bob's armored opponent was about one-hundred feet away. Then seventy. Then fifty. Then thirty. Though he couldn't see the specter's eyes, Bob knew they were locked onto his delicate cranium.

Out of the corner of his eye, Bob glanced at his right hand. His eyes grew wide as a hippo's bottom: he'd been so focused on the Black Knight, he'd forgotten to keep his own lance balanced. At this angle, his lance would miss the Black Knight completely!

The Black Knight's lance slammed into his shield. As if in slow motion, Bob felt himself lift off Jeeves' back and rocket backward. His mind raced and he scanned the area, looking for some way to knock his opponent from his horse. The Black Knight sat on his steed, unmoved, as his lance splintered against Edwina Halibut's robust heater shield.

Bob cursed himself in midair as he drew nearer to the ground. He still glared at his right hand...the hand that was gripping an in-tact lance. That was it! Whirling his wrist in a circle and swinging with all the force he could muster, Bob thrust the lance sideways, like a baseball bat.

With a crack, Bob's lance shattered against the Black Knight's helm. The armored fighter flew sideways off his saddle, the rest of his body following his head, and crashed into the dirt as Bob hit the ground. Bob groaned. Pain shot through his back muscles. Gripping his side, he stood as quickly as he was able. The Black Knight, already on his feet, unsheathed his longsword.

"Uh...what's going on, Jeeves?" Bob stuttered as the Black Knight advanced toward him.

"Both combatants have been knocked from their steeds," Jeeves explained, "According to the rules of jousting, fighters who've both fallen from their horses settle things with their swords."

27

The Black Knight's armor clinked rhythmically as, one step at a time, he drew closer to his opponent.

"But I don't have a—"

"I know, sir. I'm sorry, but there's nothing I can do. You must defeat the Black Knight using only what you have on your person."

The knight tightened his grip on the sword. Just a few more steps and he'd be within range of his unarmored opponent.

"Jeeves, how am I supposed to—"

"Sir, do you remember what you said to me before we left the house yesterday morning?"

Bob scratched his chin. "Oh!" he said.

He whipped out his laser pistol and, with three shots, knocked the Black Knight to the ground.

The two companions stared at the ancient ghost, who lay motionless on the ground. Bob's shots had punched three large holes through the breastplate, though he didn't see any blood or wounds.

"Is he dead?"

"He's been dead for over a thousand years, sir. As for his current state, I can't be sure what's going on."

Like a frog, the Black Knight hopped to his feet. Brushing the dust from his armor, he sheathed his blade and turned to Bob.

"Well played, young squire," he said, "Thou art indeed a cunning and courageous combatant. But 'tis only the first part of mine test."

In a poof of black mist, the armor-clad phantom vanished.

Panting, Bob dropped to the ground, exhausted more by fear than by combat. "What does he mean?" he said between gulps of air.

Jeeves furled his eyebrows and put his hoof to his fuzzy chin. "Before your joust…if you could call it that…the knight said that he would aid only one who was a skilled warrior and a noble soul. You've proven yourself as a warrior, sir. I suppose it's your nobility that's still in question."

Bob wiped the sweat from his forehead. "How do I prove my nobility?"

"Well sir, the castle gate is still open," Jeeves said, gesturing to the arched gateway and into the fortress beyond.

The dusty smell of antique books filled the air as Morton reorganized the bookshelf and prepared to close for the day. He pulled the curtains, darkening his Bloomsbury antique shop, and tugged on the top of the glass case to make sure it was locked.

Morton's shop contained mostly worthless knick-knacks, and most of his clientele were older ladies with little better to do than stare at antiques, but he had a few items of real value. At least, that's what the historical society had told him.

The glass case that doubled as a front desk held Morton's most valuable goods. He had a duck carved from pure gold, a tiny urn said to hold the ashes of Henry the Eighth (it didn't), a long knife thought to be hundred years old, and a shimmering ruby.

As he locked the door to the bathroom, the bell rang, signaling that someone was coming in the front door. Morton turned and saw a chubby woman around sixty years old walking with a cane. She wore a faded red shawl, an old lumpy hat, and a hand-knitted kitten sweater.

As soon as the door opened all the way, a swarm of young children crowded into the antique shop, gathering around the woman's knees. Their hair was neatly-combed and their skin was spotless. Each of the little boys wore a finely-pressed suit, shorts, and bow tie shorts and a bow tie, and the girls wore sensible dresses.

"I'm sorry, ma'am, but I was just closing up," Morton said, looking at the bizarre children.

"Oh, we won't be any trouble, dearie," the woman chittered, "We're looking for something quite specific. Aren't we, dears?"

"Yes, Nanny," The children chanted in unison.

"Alright. What, uh…what did you have in mind?" Morton stammered.

"Well, love, I think we'd like to have a look inside that case."

Quivering a little, Morton stepped behind the case and wiped the dust away. The woman's black eyes narrowed and scanned the case, coming to rest on the ruby.

"I'd be glad to take that out of the case if you'd like to look at it," Morton said

"Yes, please."

Morton's hands were quaking now. He retrieved the ruby from its case and set it on the counter. "That's one of my finest items," he stuttered, "It's hard to say for sure where it comes from, but according to legend, that ruby was one of the many gems that studded the scabbard of King Arthur's sword Excalibur."

"Really?" the woman said, a grin creeping across her face. Morton was surprised to see the stranger lift her cane, which featured the head of a dragon with scarlet eyes. As she pointed the cane toward the ruby, both the gemstone and the dragon's eyes glowed.

"That's what the historical society says," Morton said, his eyes darting to the door, "I'd be glad to wrap it up for you, Miss…"

"Morgana. But most folk just call me Nanny Le Fay. Isn't that right, little dears?"

"Yes, Nanny," the children droned once again.

"I see," Morton squeaked, taking a step back, "Would you like to pay with cash, credit, or—"

"Nothing, dearie. We'll just be taking the gemstone. Oh, and I'll need you to keep quiet about this exchange. Nosy authorities and all that."

"Quiet?" Morton stammered, his back against the wall now.

"Oh, yes. And there's no one quite as quiet as a brain-wiped man. Isn't that right, little dears?"

"Yes, Nanny," the children said. Each child reached into the folds of their clothing. They held aloft longswords, maces, morningstars, axes, daggers, broadswords, and cutlasses, each one rusty and blood-stained. One-step-at-a-time, the little urchins advanced on Morton.

"I'm terribly sorry about this, love," Nanny Le Fay said, wiping a smudge off her glasses. She raised the cane, and a beam of mystical energy shot from it. Morton collapsed onto the floor, his short-term memory erased.

Chapter 3

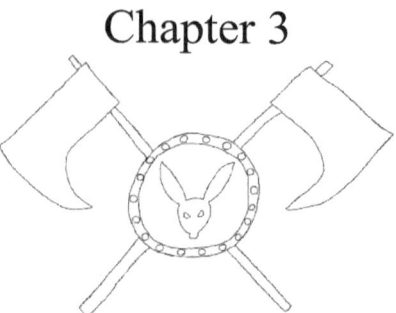

The further into the castle Bob and Jeeves strode, the darker it became. A few rays of light shot in through the narrow windows, but for the most part, the dusty, ancient stones were hidden. Choking back the dust, Bob blinked, and his eyes adjusted to the darkness.

They were in some sort of great hall. A worn, ripped, red carpet covered the floor, and on either side of the hallway were doorways leading further into the fortress. The hall was covered in tapestries, each depicting a knight on a steed. Though many were faded and aged, some of the tapestries were bright and colorful. At the bottom of each tapestry was stitched the name of the knight it depicted; names like "Perceval", "Lancelot", and "Galahad" adorned the chamber.

At the end of the hallway was a monstrous archway, and atop it was a round shield with crossed executioner's axes behind it. The shield was jet black like the Black Knight's armor, but it bore the image of a white rabbit.

"I thought this castle was ancient," Bob said, running one of the vivid tapestries through his fingers, "These look new."

"They are, sir," Jeeves said, "My micro-vision tells me the stich-work was completed recently. And judging by the distance between the stitches, the tapestries were produced by one with thick, calloused hands."

"I don't understand. Who would—"

"My guess? The Black Knight himself. Think about it, sir: what better way to pass the centuries than by creating memorials to fallen comrades and foes?"

A loud thunk pulled the pair of adventurers out of their thoughts. In the middle of the hallway stood three rectangular, black shapes obscured by the darkness. They were a little taller than Bob, and draped over each was a tapestry similar to the ones that adorned the hallway.

36

Bob heard the castle gate close behind them, and his palms grew sweaty. The darkness obscured the tapestries, but it wasn't hard to guess the purpose of the objects they covered: these were coffins.

For a moment, Bob just stared at the aged pine boxes, his face growing cold as he thought of what lay inside. Then, with a groan, the three coffins rose into the air, floating. They drifted down the hallway and into the large room beyond.

"Well," Jeeves said, clearing his throat, "At least the Black Knight is willing to help us navigate the castle. Come along, sir."

The llama trotted down the hall and into the main room with his usual, casual gait. Bob followed on the balls of his feet, glancing at the knights featured on each tapestry and wondering if he was about to come face-to-face with any of them.

The next room seemed as large as a dance hall for elephants. This room was even darker than the entrance hall and, though the walls were lined with torches, they were unlit and covered in dust and cobwebs.

37

No furniture or tapestries or paintings adorned this part of the castle. Instead, the walls, ceiling, and floor were coated in a thick blanket of ivy. Leaves and vines curled around every one of the chamber's stones, exposing only an occasional piece of the stone floor and filling the chamber with an earthy scent.

In the center of the room was a spiral staircase, which wound up through the ceiling and into next room of the castle.

Gliding just above the ivy, the trio of caskets floated straight to the stairway. Two of the pine boxes ascended the stiarcase, drifting round and round as they made their way to the next floor. The third coffin slammed into the castle floor, planting itself at the bottom of the stairway.

"What next?" Bob asked, hefting his backpack high up on his shoulders. By now, he'd learned to expect that each room of a ruin or ancient fortress would contain some sort of death trap.

"Hmmm," Jeeves said, shifting his monocle, "Unless I miss my guess, that stairway leads up the tower we saw when we first saw the castle. Our path to Excalibur lies at the top of those steps."

"And what about the ivy?"

38

"Might I suggest you avoid touching it, sir."

Tossing his head high, Jeeves continued his nonchalant trot toward the stairway. Knowing he didn't have internal sensors, Bob gingerly lowered his right foot into a clear spot between the twisting vines. So far, so good. Like a woman in new shoes walking through a dog park, Bob carefully hopped from one stone patch to another and kept his toes far from the ivy.

A series of rustling, groaning, cracking noises blasted through the chamber, and Bob snapped to attention, shooting his eyes toward his llama. There was Jeeves, covered in ivy and no longer trotting merrily through the chamber. In an instant, the plant's tentacles had shot from the castle floor and ensnared the cyber-llama.

"I believe I've made a bit of a gaffe, sir," Jeeves said through his teeth, the ivy curling around his snout like a baby's fingers, "My hoof must have brushed against one of the plants."

"Are you okay?"

"Well, my systems are becoming impaired. The vines are seeping into every conceivable crevice of my cybernetic body. And they seem to have about as much respect for my personal space as a very rude proctologist."

The torches ignited, flooding the chamber with an orange glow. Bob was motionless; he didn't dare step toward Jeeves and risk touching the ivy. Swishing noises, like the sounds of baseball bats cleaving through the air, began to echo through the chamber.

Like bubbles in lava, small, round, lumps rose from beneath the ivy. As the leaves slid away from the lumps, Bob saw patches of fur, tiny leather hoods, and fuzzy paws holding wooden poles.

They were bunnies. Petite, fuzzy, white bunnies with glittering eyes and pink ears. Each wore a black, leather cap that covered all but its eyes, and Bob could see their noses twitching beneath the canvas of vines.

Each bunny carried a long, razor-sharp executioner's axe, which they swung mechanically through the air. They crossed the room, drawing closer to the llama, and chittered gleefully, the torchlight glittering off the axe blades.

"Sir...," Jeeves muttered, glancing nervously from one executioner rabbit to the next.

Bob nodded and drew his laser pistol. His hands wobbled as he raised the weapon, trying not to draw the attention of the bunnies. Clenching his left eye shut, he aimed at one of the fuzzy lumps and fired.

The bunny slumped over, unconscious, its axe clattering to the stone floor. A dozen fuzzy heads craned toward the young adventurer. With deep-throated battle cries, the castle guardians hopped toward Bob with vengeance-fueled fury.

One of the axes arced downward, straight at Bob's face. He raised his shield. The axe head hit the shield with a clang, and Bob stumbled backward, goosestepping to keep his feet away from the ivy. Smacking the sinister bunny away, Bob grimaced as a razor-sharp axe blade sliced into his shins.

Instinctively, he whipped the pistol laser toward the rodent's head and fired, dropping the bunny warrior. Standing his ground more confidently now, he aimed at the closest approaching rabbit.

"Sir!" Jeeves shouted through clenched teeth, "Did you remember to reload since your battle with the black knight?"

Bob's heart sank like an elephant into a tub of margarine. He was almost out of plasma ammo, and the bunnies were hopping closer by the second. The energy magazine had six shots left in it when they'd left for England. He'd fired three shots into the Black Knight...two at the rabbit warriors...that left...

Bob holstered the laser pistol and licked his dry lips.

Hopping to another patch of stone-between-the-ivy, Bob ducked as a rabbit's axe sliced the hairs on the back of his neck. Another rabbit, this one standing to his left, leapt up and swung its weapon. Bob he blocked its axe strike with the shield, dropping to one knee. The first rabbit, standing beside Bob now, brought its axe level with Bob's neck, just like a tee ball player.

Thrusting his leg to the right, Bob struck the bunny with a nasty kick. He grasped around desperately and grabbed the bunny's axe just before it flew out of reach. Standing, he brought the axe down on the bunny to his left and, turned to face the approaching gang of conies.

42

More of the rabbits had reached Bob now. One struck at his back. Leaning forward, Bob let out a backward kick and sent the bunny flying. Two of them hopped at Bob, one on each side. Bob brought his axe down on the fuzzy head of one of the warriors and blocked an axe strike from the other, slashing it afterward. Bob felt a sting in his stomach as he realized what was going on: the bunnies were surrounding him.

He had to move. As cautiously as he could, Bob hopped to another patch of the stone floor, leaning back like a limbo dancer as he dodged a swinging axe. It wasn't going to work; there was no way he could make his way across the room without being ensnared by the ivy or slashed to ribbons.

Deflecting a whirring axe, Bob scanned the room, panicked. All he could focus on was the rabbits: their fuzzy, pointy ears, their adorable twitching noses and their black hoods of death. The rabbits…the rabbits that were running on top of the vines!

Like a hurdle jumper, Bob sprang forward. His foot landed squarely on one of the bunnies, which let out a surprised squeak.

43

Bounding from one hooded mammal to another, Bob bounced his way across the room.

His strange game of hopscotch eventually brought him to Jeeves, whose eye rotated to face his companion.

"Nicely done, sir," the llama said, unable to move his head or turn his neck, "Now, if you'd be so kind…"

Bob nodded and sliced a few of the vines on Jeeves' neck with the axe. Just after he worked through two of three of the strands of ivy, the plants shot up the axe's blade and then its handle.

"Let go, sir!"

Bob released the axe, watching in terror as the weapon was engulfed by the savage plants. The bunnies chattered gleefully at the revelation that their foe was unarmed. One of them sprang toward Bob, bearing its teeth as it swung its axe in a blind rodent rage.

Bob wobbled as the axe thudded into his shield, trying not to stagger backward into Jeeves. He smacked the rabbit with the shield and punted it, sending the bunny skidding across the ivy.

The rabbit popped up, joining its brethren as they closed in on their prey.

"There're too many of them, Jeeves!" Bob yelled, just beginning to notice the cold sweat on his forehead, "They'll be on us in just a minute, and I've been disarmed!"

"Have you?" Jeeves queried, shooting Bob a wry look with his right eyeball.

"I mean, I've got the laser pistol, but there's only one shot left. What are you implying?"

"Perhaps there's a solution you've overlooked. Both my fur and my suit are flame-retardant."

Bob pondered his llama's words and smiled. Drawing the revolver once again, he took careful aim at the room's stone wall.

A laser blast flew from Bob's pistol and shattered the metal structures holding one of the torches that illuminated the room. The torch dropped to the ground, igniting the ivy around it in a burst of flame. The flame spread quickly, winding throughout the plants that covered the floor like it was following a trail of gunpowder.

"It's just as I thought," Jeeves commented, "The ivy in this room looks green and healthy, but the last remnants of the castle's groundwater dried up decades ago. The plants are dry as a naked mole rat in a bathtub full of sand."

The bunnies' little eyes filled with horror. Hoisting their axes onto their backs, the little executioners made for the doorways and rabbited out of the room.

A few minutes later, Jeeves was brushing the ash from his suit jacket and Bob was scanning the ground for the axe he'd wielded.

"It's useless," he said at last, holding a stained axe head and smoldered handle between his fingers.

"I think that's the least of our concerns, sir," Jeeves commended, kneeling down. He squinted, examining Bob's legs. "That's peculiar."

"What's peculiar?"

"I saw one of those nasty little rabbits slash you across the shins. Sir, I don't see any trace of blood on you at all."

"I thought I felt something slice me there as I was fighting them."

"You don't have any burns either, sir. I should think that firestorm would have at least scorched your pant legs."

"It must just be our minds playing tricks on us."

"Indeed…"

Now that the cotton-tailed threat had passed, the treasure-hunters turned their attention back to the coffin sitting before the stairway. The box had remained untouched.

"Sir, would you like to—"

"No," Bob said, anticipating his llama's question, "No, I really don't feel comfortable doing that. Could you?"

Jeeves rolled his eyes and muttered "asinine human emotions" as he sauntered toward the casket and peeled off the tapestry.

"Oh, I'm sorry," Bob said sarcastically, "I'm sorry I have trouble disturbing the final resting place of an ancient corpse and staring at a dead body."

"Sir?"

"I'm no cold, calculating robot. Cut me some slack, llama. I just saved your hide from a bunch of axe-wielding rabbits!"

"Sir, you may want to—"

"No. Listen to me, Jeeves. I'm getting a little tired of you treating me like a moron. I've been on my share of adventures now and I think—"

"Do you have any quarters, sir?"

"What?!"

"This is no coffin."

Bob crept closer to the rectangular shape. Before him was a plastic screen contained in a man-sized metal device. Inside the rectangular box were various colorful packages, each restrained by a coiled piece of metal.

"A vending machine? Why would—?"

"I haven't the foggiest, sir. But if we're to continue our quest, I suggest we purchase some Fun Onions. Who knows? Their crunchy exterior may prove vital to solving the castle's mysteries."

The staircase stretched on and on. Bob fumbled with his laser pistol as he climbed the steps, reloading as he went. An echoing clop followed behind him as Jeeves ascended the spiral steps.

"Can you climb the stairway a little more quietly?" Bob whispered, "I don't want whatever else lives here to know we're coming."

"Oh, pish-tosh, sir. Don't tell me you don't enjoy setting off all the booby traps. It's half the fun of delving into ancient ruins."

Bob sighed and shook his head. There was no point in arguing.

Much sooner than Bob had expected, they reached the top of the staircase. They entered a round chamber about the size of Bob's kitchen. The walls were adorned with more tapestries, each featuring a minstrel playing a lute or a flute or a horn of some kind. At one end of the room, the second vending machine had embedded itself in the floor. At the other end stood a brick fireplace, which contained a small fire; it would have been homey if it wasn't so creepy.

But the first thing Bob noticed were the suits of armor. Full armor suits, each with a different design, lined the walls like silent soldiers. Their hands rested on the pommels of broadswords, which were firmly planted in the ground.

As soon as Bob and Jeeves reached the room's center, Bob heard a piece of stone slide into place. He glanced behind him and saw that the stairway had been closed-off. Then he heard the sound of armor moving.

Each of the suits of armor took a step forward, marching in unison toward the shocked adventurer and his llama. Wordlessly, the armor suits raised its swords.

"Well, sir," Jeeves said, planting his hooves, "I'd say reloading on the stairs was a wise decision."

Chapter 4

Bob smacked his tongue off the dry roof of his mouth as he glanced at the knights' blades suspended above him. He gripped the butt of his laser pistol and readied the shield. Jeeves nodded confidently. He bent his knees and took a defensive stance, studying the knights. They were surrounded, and it'd be best to let their opponents make the first move.

Bob wasn't as patient as the calculating llama. Whipping out his laser pistol, he pointed it between one of the knight's eye slits. Unfazed, the ghostly suits of armor continued their march. They were only a few feet from Bob now, and a coat of sweat pooled around the young adventurer's finger as he wrapped it around the trigger.

Then they stopped. Simultaneously, each suit of armor stopped dead in its tracks and returned to its motionless state. They had encircled the explorers, forming an oval shape with an open space to Bob and Jeeves' left. Staring into the eyeholes of the knight in front of him, Bob was confronted only with silence.

Like bipedal turtles taking jars of marmalade off a high shelf, each knight lowered its weapon and returned its sword to its original position, their palms resting on each of the weapons' pommels. One of the knights, a tall fellow wearing a spiked helmet, bent down and reached behind him. He produced a flat, square object—a piece of cardboard?—and placed it on the ground next to the pair of explorers.

Another haunted armor suit hefted a device onto its shoulders. This mechanism was metallic, about the size of a small suitcase, and featured two circles on its left and right. A series of square levers jutted out from the center of the gadget and a flat, circular dome covered the top. Inside the dome, a discus twirled round and round.

"Pardon, sir," Jeeves whispered to his shivering master, "But unless I miss my guess, that's a slightly-aged, portable music player. What do the kids call them these days?...a boom box."

The knight pressed down one of the buttons. A smooth, thumping beat erupted from the boxy bard of the '80s, and a funky melody soon followed. All at once, the knights began to move once more, bobbing side-to-side and thrusting their arms up and down. They danced with the skill of an experienced hip-hop troop.

One of the armored specters stepped forward, casting his sword aside. Bending his knees, he turned his attention to the cardboard.

"What's going on?" Bob asked, lowering his pistol.

"An ancient combat ritual, sir: the breakdancing contest."

Clamping his greaves together, the noble warrior popped and locked before diving toward the cardboard. He heaved himself up and down, wriggling his body smoothly like a dolphin gliding through the water. His armor clinked rhythmically, as if it had been forged especially for the Worm.

53

Flipping upward, the knight spread his legs and balanced himself on his palms. As his comrades pumped their armored fists with the beat, the battle-clad dancer spun on his palms, lifting his arms to let his splayed legs pass through.

Hopping onto his back, the knight thrust himself to his feet and rustled his shoulders a bit. His ghostly comrades smacked him on the back as he stood rigid once again. Turning his helmeted head to Bob, the ancient warrior extended his index finger, wordlessly issuing his challenge.

"What should I do?" Bob panted.

"Answer the challenge, sir. If we're to make any progress in our noble quest, you're going to have to bust a move."

"Can't you do it? You're full of mechanical limbs and all kinds of gizmos, aren't you?"

"Yes, sir, I do have quite the litany of 'gizmos.' But this armored fellow has challenged *you*. I can't fight this battle; it's a matter of honor."

Bob swallowed a mouthful of air as his llama gave him a firm hoof-pat on the back. "You'll do fine, sir. I have confidence in that."

Pumping his arms, thrusting his shoulders, and shimmying his legs as best he could, Bob racked his brain for images he'd once seen in music videos. For a moment, the knights continued their dancing and fist-pumping. Then they stopped, staring at the uncoordinated mess of a human before them.

Dropping to the cardboard, Bob attempted the Worm, but wound up flailing his legs and performing something in-between a push-up and the Funky Chicken. He gritted his teeth, and he tried to concentrate on his dance moves but couldn't help glimpsing at the knights surrounding him. One group of the armored soldiers shook their heads as others gave a disgusted thumbs-down.

The sounds of metal sliding against metal filled the chamber as the knights unsheathed their swords. Even as Bob tried his best to windmill, he realized it was too late. His moves had proven square and insufficient.

"Try a headspin, sir. It's the only way you'll impress these seasoned warriors."

"Are you nuts?! I could break my neck!"

"I get the sense these blokes plan to do more than that," said Jeeves as the knights raised their swords like chefs about to slice a plump carrot, "Trust me, sir!"

Placing his hands palms-down on the cardboard, Bob wobbled as he struggled to balance himself on his cranium. He bent his elbows and closed his eyes. Bob gave a firm push. And sent himself spinning like a top.

He whirled around once, then twice, then three times, and then he lost count as the world twirled round and round until it became a mass of whirring shapes.

To his shock, he felt no imbalance or pressure on his neck. Other than the nausea, the wind flying by, and the blood rushing to his head, Bob felt no discomfort whatsoever. And he wasn't losing momentum. In fact, it felt like he was speeding up.

Like the disc in the boom box, Bob became little more than a blur as he spun on the cardboard like a drill. The knights sheathed their blades and watched, speechless, as Bob flew out of his topspin and came to an abrupt stop, legs outstretched and head resting on his palm.

Shoving their fists into the air, the knights let forth a rousing cheer. Armor clanked against armor as the ancient warriors clapped and patted each other on the back and the music reached a glorious, thumping crescendo.

The noise ceased. The boom box went silent and dropped as the knights froze, then tipped over like chopped-down trees. Each suit of armor smashed against the floor, scattering pieces of armor all over the chamber.

Bob stood. "Holy cow." he finally noticed his heavy breathing amid the silence, "I never thought I could do that. I guess smooth dance moves are in my blood, eh Jeeves?"

"Not exactly, sir," the llama said, trotting over to his master and peeling something off the back of his shirt. It was a circular object made of several pieces of curved metal that rotated on their own and were connected via a golden, square base.

"It's my G-112 internal gyroscopic modulator. I thought I'd let you borrow it, sir. It makes keeping ones balance while rotating much less difficult."

Once he'd caught his breath, Bob strode over to the "coffin" that sat opposite the fireplace and ripped away the tapestry. It was another vending machine. This one contained mostly dessert items like candy bars, miniature powdered doughnuts, and fruit pies.

He shook his head and dug into his pocket, producing three quarters. The machine groaned as the age-old gears and mechanisms twisted and turned to free a Walnut Joy bar from its medieval prison.

A gust of wind blasted through the room, and the chamber went dark. The fire at the other end of the room had gone out. While Bob shoved the candy bar into his pocket with the Fun Onions, Jeeves trotted to the fireplace. He blinked five times, switching his eyeballs to night vision.

58

"Hand holds, sir," he said at last, "I've detected quite a few holes in the brick exactly the right size for one's hand or foot. Doubtless the Black Knight intends for us to climb to the next floor of the tower using the holes inside the fireplace."

"Shouldn't we wait for them to cool off first?"

"My thermal sensors aren't picking up any heat, sir. It's quite cool."

Confidently shoving his hooves into the holes in the brick, Jeeves cantered up the fireplace. Bob squinted into the holes as he remembered the rat that'd bitten his finger when he'd poked it into a crack in the stone of a pyramid.

He sighed and clambered up the fireplace. The narrow stone shaft was dim as dusk, and scattered dust particles filled his lungs. Bob plunged his hands and feet into the cold, brick handholds, one after the other, and followed his llama. At last, they reached the next floor.

The ceiling of this new room stretched high above the two adventurers, as though it were endless. Tiny beams of light streamed into the tower through the circular stone walls.

As Bob scrambled out of the brick entryway, he noticed that the enormous room had no distinct features other than a pair of statues and a sizeable stone with an anvil sitting atop it. The third vending machine was here as well, and it floated up the stone shaft toward the top of the chamber like a rectangular balloon.

Bob choked a little as he beheld the sculptures. Each was an identical cockatrice. Their elephant-sized, bat-like wings concealed their feathered bodies and their curved beaks came to a sharp point. The statues stared forward, as if guarding the stone between them and threatening all who entered the chamber with their eagle claws.

The stone appeared to be little more than a large rock, and the anvil, which looked like it had been entrenched in the stone for ages, was covered in dust. A broadsword was embedded in the anvil, as through it had been plunged into the iron tool long, long ago. The blade extended, Bob guessed, through the anvil and far into the stone. Bob examined the sword and, beneath the dust, he noticed faint carvings. He blew the dust away and read the weapon's inscription:

Whoso Pulleth Out this Sword from the Anvil

That same is Rightwise Able to Converse with the Black Knight

He took a step back from the sword and felt llama breath on his neck.

"I believe this is the moment wherein you prove your nobility, sir," Jeeves whispered as if trying not to awaken to cockatrice statues.

Bob nodded and placed his right foot against the stone. He gripped the sword with both hands and with his thumbs facing the pommel, as though he were preparing to plunge a shovel into the ground. Squaring his shoulders, Bob gave a sharp yank.

The sword didn't budge. Bob pulled once again. His arms felt like they might come out of his sockets as he strained his muscles, but the blade didn't move. On either side of the stone, Bob heard a series of cracking sounds. Groaning, he turned to look at the statues.

The stone surrounding the cockatrices had begun to crack and fall away like a shell from a hard-boiled egg. Bob could see dark red, wobbly, fleshy combs, like those of chickens, atop the creatures' heads. Their feathers were a greenish gold. Like those of a man awakened out of a sound sleep, the mammoth birds' eyes shot open, revealing their yellow eyes.

Bob released his grip on the sword and reached for his laser pistol only to spot dozens of stones floating into view. One by one, each stone that made up the chamber's floor was detaching itself and drifting upward like a balloon. With a rumble, the boulder he stood on shook itself free of the chamber's floor and rose into the air.

Jeeves rocked back and forth. Each of his hooves was resting on a different stone and, as they began to float, he'd become imbalanced. The rock had fallen away from the cockatrices completely now, and one unfurled its wings, flapping and letting out a fearsome caw.

The cyber-llama ignited his rectum rocket and, with a blast of fire, took to the air. The time for stealth had passed.

Like a bottle rocket, the truck-sized bird shot from its perch. Its beak snapped at the space where Jeeves had been half a second ago as the llama weaved around its feathery hide and activated his laser vision, zapping the cockatrice on the side of the face.

The bird howled and struck with its claws. Jeeves dove downward, blasting the mythical fowl with his lasers once again. The cockatrice was fast, but couldn't quite match cyber-llama engineering.

Bob steadied himself as he stood on the large boulder that held the anvil. The other monstrous bird beat its wings in-rhythm, keeping pace with the rising stone that held the sacred sword. Its eyes were locked on its chubby, human prey, and Bob bent his knees, waiting for the beast to strike.

The cockatrice cawed and swiped at Bob with its mighty claws. Bob leapt to a nearby series of hovering stones, teetering as the stones flew up the tower. Bob thrust out his arms to keep from falling, and the straps of his backpack slipped off. The backpack fell, landing on a floating stone dozens of feet below the young adventurer.

Wrenching open its beak once again, the enormous birdie nipped at its quarry. Bob ducked limbo-style, raising his laser pistol and shooting the cockatrice in the chin. The bird raised its head, screeching like Yoko Ono with a bullhorn. The bird seemed more annoyed than hurt as it drew its head level with the human explorer's and stared into Bob's eyes.

Zotting the cockatrice with his laser vision gave Jeeves a chuckle, but it didn't seem to be harming the ancient bird. A smell like seared chicken reached Jeeves' nostril sensors as the bird prepared for another attack. The bird slashed at the llama again and again as Jeeves ducked and dodged around the chamber.

He blasted off into one direction with the cockatrice hot on his hooves. The llama led the cockatrice around the chamber, and the two looked like a pair of battling remote-control planes. Jeeves abruptly shut off the rectum rocket, flying backward with his hoof extended and hitting the cockatrice between the eyes.

As the bird recovered, Jeeves racked his databanks for a way to harm the birds. Although their feather-covered flesh was sensitive, it was thick and tough. A bit lost in thought, Jeeves failed to notice the pair of talons bearing down on him.

The cockatrice at last grabbed hold of its prey. It began to squeeze, digging its talons into the four-legged intruder. As his gears and metallic innards cracked and snapped, Jeeves prayed his young companion was having better luck.

Bob bounded backward, his back touching the large stone. He felt the tip of the cockatrice's claw rip through his shirt and scrape his stomach. He ignored the pain and the blood that trickled out and took aim with his laser pistol once again, this time shooting the bird squarely in the eye.

The cockatrice clenched its eye shut, jutting its wing outward and smacking the annoying human. Bob lost his footing and tumbled across the floating stones, landing none-too-gently on a series of brick-shaped rocks.

He raised his shield as the colossal fowl's beak bore down on him once again. It smashed against the shield with a clang, driving the floating stones further into Bob's back. Shifting his right arm, the one that held the laser pistol, beneath the shield, Bob shot the bird in the stomach. The cockatrice stumbled back, giving Bob time to stand.

Wounding the creature in the stomach gave Bob time to think. The pistol's blasts weren't powerful enough to penetrate the beast's thick hide. Shooting it would keep it at bay until he ran out of shots, but there had to be a way to kill the blasted birds.

He remembered the sharpened slab of rock he'd used to fight a giant armadillo during his trip to Mexico. Bob holstered his laser pistol, reached to his right, and plucked one of the drifting stones from the air. As the savage bird recovered from its injury, Bob held the stone in front of him, gripping it…like a sword. Just like he would have held a sword.

Grinning, Bob released the brick and fixed his sights on the sword in the stone and anvil a few yards away. Like a child playing "the floor is lava," Bob hopped from one stone to another, making a beeline for the ancient sword.

The cockatrice's talons continued to crush the llama. Jeeves grimaced as he thought of the blood and oil stains he'd have to clean out of his suit jacket once he got home. The cockatrice let forth a victory caw and spread its wings wide, flying upward with its quarry.

Another internal gear shifted out of place, and the llama winced. He had to escape the bird's grasp before his innards became little more than llama goop.

Shifting just a little, Jeeves kicked with his front hooves. He felt the cockatrice stumble a bit as its grip on the llama weakened. Jeeves peeked over his shoulder and smiled; his body was angled downward now and his derriere, still in the bird's claws, was pointed upward, straight at the monster's wing. The llama warrior ignited the rectum rocket.

Flame shot from Jeeves' behind and onto the bird's canvas-like wing. The cockatrice shrieked, releasing Jeeves and flailing around the chamber, trying to put out the flame.

Once he'd reached a safe distance from the creature, Jeeves hovered in place and caught his breath. The bird, though now focused on its flaming wing, was no less dangerous. There had to be a way to seriously wound these things.

The sound of wings thrashed behind him as Bob reached the stone and anvil. He placed his right foot on the stone and gripped the sword hilt once again. This time, he grasped the sword with his thumbs pointed downward toward the blade, less like he was using a butter churn and more like he was wielding a broadsword.

Like a butter knife cutting through lime gelatin, the blade slid out of the stone and anvil. Bob held the sword aloft and faced the cockatrice. The one-eyed bird scowled at the adventurer, its beak half-open as it seethed.

The bird brought its beak down, smacking Bob's shield once again. Bob slashed the bird across the chest, leaving a deep cut. The cockatrice screamed. Its left claw shot toward Bob, and then the right, as the bird tried to slash its nemesis apart.

Bob hopped over the left claw and, landing on the beast's right leg, sprang upward, plunging his blade straight into the creature's heart. The massive wings stopped flapping and the cockatrice dropped. With one final, panicked squawk, the monster breathed its last.

Bob placed his foot on the animal's ribcage for leverage and yanked the broadsword out.

Another thundering caw startled Bob, and his eyes darted to the other cockatrice. The second bird had a large burn mark on its left wing, but the fire had gone out and the monster appeared unharmed. The bird glared at Jeeves and dove toward the cybernetic llama.

At the speed of thought, Bob skipped across the floating stones toward the colossal bird. Just before the monster's outstretched talons reached the injured llama, Bob slammed into it shield-first, ramming the bird against the tower's stone wall.

The cockatrice rolled, pushing the sword-wielder off its belly, and stood upright. Bob crouched, slashing at the bird's legs, but the cockatrice avoided the strike with a quick hop. Dodging the beast's beak, Bob tried to stab the cockatrice as he had the first one, but the bird was too quick and the human was becoming tired.

A flash of red light hit the bird in the side of the face as Jeeves' laser vision hit its mark. The creature's neck craned and its glance shot toward Jeeves. Bob saw his opportunity and brought his sword down on the beast's neck, lopping off the cockatrice's head.

As soon as the bird's head dropped, Bob felt a jerk as the chamber's stones stopped rising. Like a jigsaw puzzle, each of the stones came to a stop at the top of the tower, fitting together to form the room's floor once again.

Bob could see the ceiling this time, as well as the stone and anvil and the vending machine. Hefting the backpack onto his shoulders, Bob grasped his stomach and crept toward Jeeves.

"Can I have some bandages, Jeeves?" he asked, showing the llama the slash wound on his stomach.

"Indeed," Jeeves said, pulling some gauze from his chest compartment and watching his master quizzically as Bob patched up his wounds.

Now that the battle was won, Bob and Jeeves examined their new surroundings. On the side of the room opposite the stone and anvil stood a curved, wooden door. In the center of the door was an iron doorknocker in the shape of a hand grasping a bejeweled sword. Though the wood that made up the door was bent with age, Bob somehow knew the door was sturdy.

He reached for the doorknocker when Jeeves stopped him. "Sir, don't you think it best if we examine the third vending machine before proceeding?"

Bob nodded and snatched the tapestry from the third snack dispenser. This one was a soda machine and, grumbling, Bob inserted his quarters and selected a Big C cola (it was 25 cents cheaper.) He shoved the cold can into his pocket and raised the door knocker, rapping on the door.

The door creaked with age and slid open. The room beyond was well-lit; torchlight danced on the stone walls, revealing the ancient treasures beyond. Shields, axes, swords, spears and other weapons, as well as piles of golden coins and suits of armor, were strewn haphazardly across the floor.

In the center of the room was a tall, wooden chair, intricately carved with images of knights on horseback. The figure who sat on the chair was hard to make out in the torchlight, but Bob soon heard a familiar voice:

"Thou hast proven thyself a noble soul," the Black Knight said, rising from the chair and striding toward Bob, "Now I shall give to thee my counsel."

"Uh...thanks," Bob stammered, blinking a few times, "Come on, Jeeves."

"Wait!" The Black Knight bellowed, raising his hand and motioning for Bob to stop, "Hast thou brought an offering?"

Bob scratched his head. "Yes," he said at last, stowing his sword and shield and reaching into his pockets, "I hath brought thee an offering of Fun Onions, Walnut Joy, and Big C."

"Big C?!" The knight shouted, "Dost thou dare bring unto me a generic brand?! I shouldst smite thee where thou stand for thy insolence. But then, not many can brave the trials of my castle. Step into my chamber, warrior, and bring thy offering."

Chapter 5

The fire atop the torches quivered in judgment as Bob and his quadruped companion stepped into the Black Knight's study. It was warmer than the rest of the castle and a little cramped. As they neared the wooden throne, the ancient ghost sat and gestured for Bob and Jeeves to do the same.

Bob squeezed himself between a pile of gold coins and a blood-stained halberd and eyed at the Black Knight. The knight returned Bob's gaze. His right hand still held the "offering" of snacks and, bringing his hands together with a precision worthy of any master of combat, tore the Fun Onions open with one, swift motion.

He lifted the front of his helmet just enough to make room for his fingers and delicately lifted one the flaky, crunchy treats to his lips. Rhythmic crunching followed. The Black Knight dipped his fingers into the bag once again, producing another single Fun Onion. One by one, he emptied the bag and soon, his armor was covered in tiny, salty flecks.

Then he produced the blue bar of walnut and coconut, pinching the end and peeling away the plastic like he was eating a sugary banana. The only sound the two adventurers cold hear was the flickering of the torchlight. Jeeves shifted uncomfortably. Bob cleared his throat.

"I don't mean to be rude, but can you please explain--"

"Silence!" the Black Knight bellowed, "My sacred rituals shall not be interrupted for any mortal man!"

Bob shut his mouth, and the ancient warrior continued carefully unwrapping his candy bar. After fifteen separate bites and thirty dignified sips of Big C, the Black Knight let forth a mighty belch and sighed, patting his armored belly.

"Many thanks, good fellows," he said, moving his helmet's face plate back into place, "Mine munchy trove was depleted centuries ago. I hath not craved sweet and salty things so much since the great Babylonian Cool Ranch Chip famine of 1483."

"You're welcome," Bob said, tugging on his shirt collar.

"Good sir knight," Jeeves piped up, "Your company is indeed refreshing, but might you give us a few more details about Excalibur? We're in the midst of a quest, after all."

"Indeed. I envy you, young ones, able to venture across the land pursuing treasure. I hath been trapped in this castle for so long, I scarcely remember the feel of grass beneath mine feet or the sound of a dachshund yodeling in the moonlight. Simply trapped here, whiling away the hours, and guarding that blasted sword."

"You've been here since the days of Camelot?" Bob asked, leaning forward.

"Yes, good sir. In those days, I was called Pellinore. A deposed king was I, confined to this castle after Arthur was appointed high king of all Britannia. When Arthur approached mine castle and we first battled, I smote his sword in twain and thought at last my revenge was nigh.

"But the king was spirited away by the magician Merlin and soon returned with the mystical sword Excalibur. Our battle was fierce as any Black Friday mall rush, but at last, Arthur disarmed me. To my amazement, the king spared my life and commanded that I join his Knights of the Round Table."

Here the knight paused, raising his head and looking into nothingness. "Our quests were noble and our parties swanky, we Knights of the Round Table. But all must come to an end, I suppose. The sinister knight Sir Mordred tricked Arthur into a long journey and seized control of Camelot for himself. My companions and I fought long and hard against the traitors, but in the end, we were overwhelmed. I myself met my end upon a spearhead just outside Camelot's walls.

"But to my shock, I found my soul peeling away from my body like Play-Dough from a fun factory; I was floating high above the ground in a ghostly form. Unable to control mine momentum, I floated for miles until at last I came upon a lake with

77

a slender maiden standing atop it. And in her hands was Excalibur, the king's blade.

"She said unto me that I had been chosen to keep watch over the sword, to ensure that the powerful blade came not into evil hands. For now, the soggy mystic foretold, I wouldst be confined to my old castle, unable to leave its walls. But should Excalibur ever be pursued by a sinister force, I wouldst be permitted to leave the castle and aid in its recovery."

Sir Pellinore leaned in, his eye slits resting on Bob, "Your presence means but one thing: evil is afoot once again. Some vile presence seeks the king's sword."

Bob felt his heartbeat speed up as he unsheathed the sword he'd pulled from the stone. "Is this it?" he asked.

"No. Though a fine blade it is, the same sword that accompanied me on countless adventures in my youth. It is yours, if you wish. I fear that locating Excalibur will be far more perilous. Any foe able to steal from the Lady of the Lake is one not to be trifled with."

"I'm not so sure about that, good sir knight," Jeeves said, brushing some stray Fun Onion crumbs from his suit jacket, "I know the lady was a wise force of nature back in her day, but of late she has become...well...a few Smuurfs short of a mushroom village.

"I see." Sir Pellinore drummed his fingers against the chair's armrest as he placed an armored hand on his chin, "Then I fear I may not prove much help after all. If I were to get near a place where Excalibur once was, I may be able to sense it, but without a hint of any sort, the blade is lost."

Bob cast his head downward in thought, but soon raised his eyebrows. "Jeeves, didn't you say Grandma Edwina won the scabbard from the Lady in a poker game?"

"Indeed I did, sir."

"Then the Lady of the Lake developed a gambling problem in her later years?"

"I'm afraid so. I recall Edwina describing to me the countless shouts of 'I must send word to my bookie!' during her adventures with the Lady."

79

"So isn't it possible she gambled away Excalibur itself in the same way she lost the scabbard to Grandma?"

Jeeves smiled. "Now that's a Halibut brain in action, sir. To the gambling dens of London!"

"Fantastic!" the Black Knight chimed in, "At last, I shall leave this accursed castle. Come, we shall take the elevator."

"Madam, we don't allow children in here."

"Oh, but the little dears do so love the spinning slot machines and the fine clothes of the resident gamblers. Don't you, children?"

"Yes, Nanny."

The series of well-dressed children stood like soldiers in front of the roulette table, concealing their weapons. The soft voice of Nanny Le Fay was almost impossible to hear through the pinging and beeping and booping of the casino games.

"I understand that a day at the casino can make for a jolly good time," the security guard said, twisting his bow tie and shuddering as he peeked behind Le Fay at the long row of expressionless children, "But I've got to enforce the rules. You and your children are going to have to leave."

"You know what would be grand?" Nanny said, taking a step closer to the security guard and twisting the corners of her mouth into a smile, "If we could get a tour of the owner's office. I'm sure he's got lots of trophies and colorful poker chips and all sorts of lovely things. Wouldn't that be grand, dears?"

"Yes, Nanny," the children chanted.

The guard's expression hardened and his hand drifted toward his taser. Reaching into her purse, Nanny Le Fay produced a leather pouch that featured the glowing image of a brain with outstretched hands closing around it. She poured out a handful of powder and, like she was blowing the seeds off a dandelion, blew the stuff into the guard's face.

"What do you think you're--" The man stiffened as the color faded from his eyes and was replaced by a fiery orange glow. His skin became pale and dry, and his mouth hung agape.

"Take us to the manager's office," Le Fay said, more sternly this time.

Wordlessly, the security guard shuffled away from the roulette table and toward the back of the casino. Nanny turned around.

"You see, children? All it takes to achieve your goals is a little persistence."

"Just how many casinos have we visited this afternoon, sir?"

"Fourteen."

"And, just so I can properly record it in my memory banks, how many mystic, ancient swords have we found?"

"I'm not in the mood, Jeeves. It's been a long day."

"You may want to tell that to the man who's been stuck in the same castle for a few centuries, sir."

The shaking of dice, shuffling of cards, spinning of the roulette table, plinking of coins, and occasional swearing blurred together into a deafening din as Bob and his llama trudged through the windowless building. Lights flashed all around them, and the spinning cherries, lemons, and sevens in the slot machines were beginning to make Bob queasy.

"Black Knight...I mean, Sir Pellinore," Bob piped up, "Do you sense anything here?"

"Hmmm...I shall take mine bearings now," said a voice next to Bob. After that heart attack incident at the bingo parlor forty-five minutes ago, the threesome had thought it best if the Black Knight made himself completely invisible while in public. As his invisible friend meditated to sense of his connection to the ancient sword, Bob scanned the casino, wondering how long it would take security to notice the well-dressed llama.

"Aha!" the Black Knight said at last, "I hath sensed my destiny: chicken wings, Buffalo-style if I'm not mistaken. Twenty paces to the left. And a sea of ranch dressing that Erik the Red himself could not conquer. Oh, and Excalibur's been here, too."

Bob's face brightened. "It's here?"

"No, young squire, the blade hath *been* here. But now that we've drawn closer to it, it shall not be too difficult a task for me to find the hand that hath wielded that blade. After I've taken in some sustenance, of course."

A wisp of air brushed against Bob's arm as the ancient warrior left his side. It wasn't long before Bob spotted a floating plate of chicken wings moving toward him. The meat gradually disappeared off each one, reducing it to a bone.

"Now, to adventure and glory!" the Black Knight shouted, spraying half-chewed chicken across the casino floor.

The plate of poultry glided forward, and Bob crept behind it, glancing at all the casino patrons too engrossed in their games to notice the ghostly activity. After weaving around a roulette table, the three adventurers came at last to a posh office.

Through the open door, Bob spotted a mahogany desk with a wheeled, red chair behind it. Plaques and awards coated the walls and, in the corner, a television blared. The desk itself held a sleek, black phone and several bobble-heads. Two slender security guards, each donning a black suit and dark glasses, stood behind it.

Seated in the chair was a mustached man in a clean, white suit with enough grease in his hair to lubricate a jet engine. In one

84

hand he held a cane with a handle that resembled a dragon's head. The slender fellow nodded and cocked one of his eyebrows.

One of the security guards marched toward the intruders, but the man behind the desk swiveled in his chair and whipped his cane upward, stopping the guard.

"Come on in, guys," he said, standing to greet his guests, "It's always a pleasure to entertain guests of the casino. Gamblers. Partakers in games of chance. The kind of guys who would spank a buffalo with a wooden paddle for the heck of it...you know."

"Thank you, my good man," Jeeves said, trotting into the office, "But I'm afraid we haven't come to enjoy your establishment's facilities. We've come in search of information. You are Mr. Stickyfingers, the owner of this establishment, yes?"

Bob warily followed his llama into the office. With a click, the door closed behind him, and the noise of the casino faded away.

"Daniels, get our friends a Big C Cola, would you?" Mr. Stickyfingers said, gesturing to one of the muscular guards and leaning against the desk, "Yeah, that's me. Stickyfingers. Casino owner. Millionaire. Proud wearer of blue footie pajamas...you know."

"Indeed," Jeeves said, nodding in thanks to one of the security guards as he lifted a cola glass with his mechanical tentacle, "My name is Jeeves, and this is Bob Halibut. We'd like to inquire about a transaction you had with a very...unique woman some years ago."

The other security guard handed Bob a full glass. As he lifted the beverage to his lips, Bob sniffed it and frowned. Tipping his glass, he let a bit of the liquid spill onto the floor. The drink sizzled and popped as the floor beneath it crumbled away. Bob stared wide-eyed at the drink in his llama's hand.

"A unique woman?" Stickyfingers said as he tossed the dragon's head cane from one hand to the other, "A wacky bird? A strange dame? One of those wonky grandmas? Now what would I have had to do with someone like that?"

"You're a gambler, are you not?"

"You've got me pegged, llama."

"Do you recall playing a game against a slender, black-haired woman a bit...moist?"

Stickyfingers thought for a bit and a smile spread across his lips. He walked behind the desk, scratching his whiskery chin. Bob curled his fingers around the hilt of his sword.

"Oh, I think I know what you're gettin' at." Stickyfingers' voice grew higher. "I knew somebody'd be on my tail. It's an honor to finally see you gents. Hello, Pellinore."

Bob and Jeeves stiffened, and Bob tightened his grip on his weapon. "There's no need for us to keep hiding, my dear," Stickyfingers continued, his voice growing higher now, "I just want to chat. As one old friend to another."

The black, transparent helmet wobbled into view and, one by one, each piece of the black armor appeared until a fully-armored knight stood before the casino owner. Stickyfingers lifted his cane with both hands and tapped the floor.

In an instant, his taught skin mushroomed out, becoming wrinkly and flabby, and his tall frame shrunk and bended. Before the adventurers stood an elderly woman in a hand-knit sweater and shawl. If he hadn't known better, Bob might have expected her to offer him fresh-baked cookies.

Though he'd never seen the Black Knight's face, Bob knew Pellinore was scowling. "Le Fay," he sneered.

"You're as pleasant as ever, dearie," the old woman said, "Though I must admit to just a bit of envy. The years haven't been as kind to me. Anti-aging spells work better than your average wrinkle cream, but they're no Fountain of Youth."

"You deserve every wrinkle," the Black Knight grumbled.

The old woman sighed, plopping into the chair and spinning around. "You never were the fun-loving type. But don't be un-gallant, sir knight. Introduce me to your companions."

The Black Knight whirled toward Bob. "Draw your blade, squire," he said, unsheathing his own sword, "Before you is Morgana Le Fay: master sorceress, treacherous sister of King Arthur, and the bane of all Camelot."

"You forgot 'snappy dresser' and 'three-time pie-baking contest winner,' old friend. These old bones could use a few more compliments, you know."

"Where is Mr. Stickyfingers?" Bob said, surprised by the sound of his own voice.

"The casino owner?" Morgana laughed, "Well, let's see...my memory's not what it used to be. But I believe that, since this morning, he's been tumbling through another dimension. It's not as hard to open a portal for such things as one might think.

"But he knew the risks of the gambling business. Isn't that right, little dears?"

"Yes, Nanny."

Like a seahorse laying eggs, the stomachs of the security guard suits burst open and a series of children straight out of a Stephen King novel filed out. Each carried a sword, morningstar, or other weapon and stared, expressionless, at the llama, the ghost, and Bob.

Le Fay wobbled to her feet and fumbled with her cane. She twisted the dragon's head around, and a red glow shot from the dragon's eyes.

"It's been lovely catching up. But I'm afraid I have errands to run. You know, fetching an ancient sword and enacting a new age of darkness and all that. Goodbye, my dears."

A plume of purple smoke erupted from the floor as the octogenarian warlock vanished. In unison, the clean-cut children raised their weapons and dashed toward the adventurers. Drawing his shield, Bob blocked a spear thrust, which launched him through the office door and into a poker table. Chips and cards scattered as two of Morgana's whelps leapt at their quarry.

Rolling to one side, Bob spotted a pile of poker chips lying on the ground. Like a golfer, he swatted the chips with his sword, sending them flying into one of the children's faces. The second child scowled at Bob and, wordlessly, hopped toward him and struck with her flail. Bob dropped to one knee as he raised his shield and deflected the strike.

"What do we do, Jeeves?" Bob panted as panicked casino patrons flew past him, "Evil guinea pigs and conquistadors are one thing, but we can't fight children!"

Jeeves shot from the room and dropped to the carpet as an arrow whizzed over his head and embedded itself in a roulette wheel. "A noble sentiment, sir, one that your grandmother would be proud of. In fact, I recall that, just after I was constructed, Edwina took me to her basement, placed my hoof on a Bible, and made me take an oath."

The llama spat at the three spear-wielding children who approached him, deploying a smoke bomb. "The oath had many tenets, but one was that I never, under any circumstances, seriously hurt a child. Children, your grandmother explained, are innocent, impressionable little doves and have the potential to grow into anything."

Bob leapt out of the way of a scimitar strike. The little boy's sword hit a blackjack table instead, splitting it in two. "So what can we do?!"

"Your earlier statement was only half-correct, sir," Jeeves explained, "You and I are adventuring heroes, above vile practices like injuring of young ones. We must never, *ever* seriously hurt children. But that doesn't mean we can't smack them around a bit in self-defense."

Balancing on his front hooves, Jeeves shot his rear hooves backward, lightly smacking his pursuers in the face and sending them to the ground.

"Take that, innocent little doves."

Bob nodded and spun his sword, exposing the flat of the blade. Whirling the blade downward, he whacked the flail-wielding girl into a pile of playing cards and wheeled around to parry a strike from the boy's sword.

The children's archer emerged from the office and nocked another arrow, aiming at the furry thing that had kicked his brethren. He smirked as he released the bowstring and heard the whine of the arrow in flight. With a clank, the arrow flew off course, as if it were deflected by an unseen force. The black suit of armor flashed into view, and the Black Knight flew toward the surprised young henchman.

The small child jumped up and twirled in midair, performing a roundhouse kick. He hit the Black Knight square in the helmet and landed with his fists clenched, bobbing up-and-down like a boxing champ. Enraged, Pellinore swung with the flat of his blade, but his opponent raised his forearm, blocking the blade and kicking the Black Knight in the stomach. His armor dented, Pellinore sheathed the sword and punched at his opponent. The kid dodged right, straight into the Black Knight's uppercut, and flew sprawling across the office desk.

The smack of Bob's blade disarmed another of the creepy children, but more and more came streaming from the casino office. Bob blocked one strike after another, but gradually, the savage youngsters pushed their opponent toward the slot machines. He tightened the straps of his backpack and frowned. He had time for only a quick peek behind him, but Bob knew if he tried to navigate the levers and flashing lights of the slot machine hallway, the children would cut him to ribbons. His left arm ached as a morningstar bounced off his shield and an axe blade cut his cheek, narrowly missing his jaw.

Like a leaping jaguar, a little boy wielding two hand axes vaulted above his fellow warriors. Turning pale at the sight of the airborne child, Bob spotted the large chandelier behind him and a spark of inspiration surged through his brain like a lizard running on two legs across scorching desert sands.

Bob's llama was facing his own horde of youngsters just outside the office door. Jeeves cricked his furry neck, causing five bean bag cannons to slide from his ribcage. The seven children approaching him whined as the bean bags thudded against them, but they continued forward. Jeeves glowered. He was slowing the little monsters, but not stopping them. As the bean bags continued flying toward the kids, the llama caught sight of a short girl with a battle axe. Swinging it in a circle in front of her, like a propeller, she sliced each bean bag as she inched closer to her prey.

Raising the weapon above her shoulder, the girl arced the weapon toward Jeeves. The metal plates in his chest slid out of the way as one of Jeeves' many metallic cannons popped from his chest. Steadying himself, Jeeves blasted the girl's weapon with his

94

bubble gum cannon, covering the deadly blade with pink goo. The girl was thrown off balance, and Jeeves took the opportunity to yank his G-112 gyroscopic modulator out of place and smack the young child. The girl spun around and revealed the left side of her axe blade, which was soon covered in bubble gun. The mechanical quadruped made sure to coat her hands with the sticky, pink substance as well.

Jeeves activated the modulator. As Bob had during the break-dancing contest, the girl began to twirl round and round, turning green. Completely out of control, she spun toward her fellow child warriors. The children dispersed and ran like exposed cockroaches as the gum-covered blades smacked them over and over, flinging them to the ground. By the time one of the children had the sense to pull the gyro off his companion's back, the llama was nowhere to be seen.

Inside the casino owner's office, the kid jumped to his feet, plunging his hand into the desk drawer and pulling out a pair of long daggers. The Black Knight tightened his grip on the sword and darted into the office. The child whirled the knives around, bending his knees and bracing to face his opponent.

The Black Knight blocked strike after strike. He was rusty (in more ways than one), and the child was a quick opponent. As he blocked a dagger strike and tried to whack his opponent with his shield, Sir Pellinore shook his head, attempting to clear his mind and remember his training.

Back in the days when he was Prince Pellinore, he'd been taught to be alert, always to gauge his opponent and to find a weakness. As the child dodged his sword strikes, the Black Knight remembered the many mock battles he'd fought, the day he received the sword that young Master Halibut now wielded, and the knighting ceremony on his twenty-first birthday, when he'd had...when he'd had his first taste of sugar water!

Hopping away from his opponent, Pellinore sheathed his blade and barreled toward the drink station. Grabbing a bottle of cola by the neck, he flung it onto the desk, smashing it open and splashing cola everywhere. The child backed up. The daggers clattered to the floor as a cold sweat overtook the little tyke.

"What's the matter, young squire?" Pellinore mocked.

"Nanny says...," the boy stuttered, "Nanny says that good little boys and girls aren't to sneak sugary drinks from grown-ups. Those drinks are for adults."

The black-clad warrior grabbed two more bottles and popped the tops off. Soda drizzled onto the carpet as the Black Knight marched toward the terrified youngster. He smirked as he thought of Le Fay's sick sense of irony; the twisted lessons she taught these kids would be her undoing. He was almost atop the child now, who sat, quivering, in the corner.

"Leave," Pellinore said.

The little boy dashed for front door, goose-stepping across the carpet to avoid the pools of booze.

Bob fixed his eyes on the leaping boy with the axes as he raised his shield, blocked several strikes, and focused. Jumping himself, Bob whirled the broadsword like a gymnastics ribbon and brought it down on the little boy's hands, swatting his wrists. The child wasn't cut, but yelped and released his grip on the hand axes.

97

Bob stowed the heater shield behind his back and grabbed one of the small axes. Like he was throwing a discus, he hurled the axe straight toward the chandelier.

The axe hit its mark. The flying blade sliced through the thin, flexible chord that held up the ceiling decoration. The chandelier dropped like a walrus off a high dive and smashed into the floor, sending expensive glass scattering across over the casino. At the sound of the crash, the children instinctively whipped around. Bob saw his opportunity, spun on his heels, and sprinted down the hallway, slot machines on either side.

It didn't take long for the children to realize that their prey was escaping. Bob had scarcely made it to the end of the row of gambling machines before the children began to pursue him, brandishing their weapons and gritting their teeth. Bob shoved the sword into his belt and drew his laser pistol. He took a deep breath to keep his hands from shaking. His accuracy had to be perfect.

He pulled the trigger. The padlock on the front of the slot machine to his left popped off, and the front door flew open, spilling coins all over the carpet. Bob took aim at another slot machine and fired again, pouring a second load of twenty pence pieces on the hallway's carpet. Soon, six slot machines had burst and the hall was covered in piles of silver-colored coins.

The children at the front of the charge tried to stop themselves but were pushed by the kids behind them. They plowed into the piles of coins, tripping and smashing into them and scattering pence all over the floor. The children cried in frustration as they clambered over each other and peeled the coins off their skin, desperately trying to stand.

Pushing the air out of his cheeks, Bob raised his hand to his cheek, expecting the cold trickle of blood from the axe that had brushed his face. But there was no wound. Bob's llama zipped to his side, switching off the rectum rocket just as he reached his master.

"Good work, sir. But I'm not sure how long your little ruse will keep these children at bay. Hop on."

"But we still don't know where Excalibur is!" Bob panted.

"As usual, sir, you're wrong. Our knight friend has located a clue to the sword's location. Now, if you please, sir, hop on."

Bob nodded and leapt into the llama's back. Jeeves blasted through the casino doors, leaving singe marks and groaning children in his wake.

At first, Bob thought he might take a rest from battle and take in the sights as they zipped around the streets of London. He soon gave up. Screaming pedestrians jumped out of the way as the llama weaved between the city's buildings, his legs up against his underbelly.

Bob gripped his llama's fur and choked back a little vomit, a plastic bag brushing against his face. "Mind telling me where we're going?"

"I heard from Pellinore just before we left, sir, that as he battled one of those ghastly youngsters in Stickyfingers' office, he encountered a curious piece of parchment. If you please, Black Knight, make yourself visible and show our young friend your discovery."

A black, armored hand materialized to Jeeves' left, keeping pace with the soaring llama. It gripped a pink pamphlet, which Bob snatched. Holding it with both hands as it flapped in the wind, Bob squinted and read the words "Society of Pelican Groomers: Welcome New Inductee."

"What does this mean, Pellinore?" he shouted over the blasts of wind.

"Thou knowest not of the Society of Pelican Groomers?" the voice next to Bob said, "I hath been locked in mine castle for centuries and even I know of those blue bloods who buffer the birds. 'Tis the most exclusive society of antique collectors and pelican washers in the world."

"The society is famous for its exclusivity," said Jeeves, "The only way for a new member to join the Pelican Groomers' ranks is to bring an antique of incredible value to add to their collection."

"Excalibur!" Bob cried.

"Precisely, sir. Mister Stickyfingers must have recently joined the society and, I suspect, used the ancient sword as his entry fee. The Society of Pelican Groomers is currently managed by Lady Floofenshire of Kensington and meets at her mansion every Tuesday afternoon. I just pray we can reach Kensington before Le Fay gets her wrinkly hands on the sword...and on Lady Floofenshire."

Chapter 6

The afternoon breeze brushed against Lady Floofenshire's billowy dress as the sun streamed into her parlor. She was sitting in the big, leather chair, as she did nearly every afternoon, picking flecks of dust off her pet pelican, Percy, and admiring her antiques. Ceramic dolls, vases, hand-painted teapots, finely-woven Persian rugs, phonographs of all sizes, and other treasures adored her parlor.

On her lap next to Percy was Floofenshire's latest treasure: a longsword, dusty but still as sharp as the day it was forged. The hilt was coated with pure gold, though it bore no scuff marks, and jewels of all colors were set across the hand guard, grip, and pommel. The sun glistened off the gems and nearly blinded the collector. Carvings of knights, dragons, trolls, and other medieval creatures covered the hilt. The blade bore a few such engravings and, curiously, the carvings were not worn. Lady Floofenshire chuckled. Excalibur indeed.

There was a knock at the front door. Lady Floofenshire set her new sword and her pelican on the chair and peeked through the peephole. She saw a bent-over woman, much older than she, with a well-dressed boy and girl standing like statues around her knees. Lady Floofenshire bit her thumbnail. She should wait for Stevens to answer the door, just to be safe. Still, what harm could there be in letting an octogenarian and two adorable children in the house?

She eased the door open. "Hello there. How can I help you?"

"Good afternoon, Lady Floofenshire," the old woman said, leaning on her cane, "The little dears and I were out for an afternoon stroll when the children peeked in your front window and began admiring your antique collection. We were wondering if you might be willing to give us a closer look. Weren't we, children?"

"Yes, Nanny," the pair of children droned.

"Well, uh," the lady stammered, "That's a strange request. One doesn't generally just invite strangers into their home. I must take steps to ensure my safety, you understand."

"Absolutely, my dear. I understand. It's just that we'd heard of your generosity and your exquisite collection and were hoping to get a peek. But I suppose safety does come first. Come, children."

Lady Floofenshire cleared her throat. "No, wait. You can come in for a quick peek. I don't see the harm."

A warm smile spread across the old woman's face. "Oh thank you, my dear!"

The two children and their nanny shuffled into Lady Floofenshire's mansion, and the elderly woman herded the children out of the entryway and into the parlor. The Lady smiled and shut the door with a click. She didn't notice the little boy darting toward her windows and closing the shutters. As soon as the afternoon sun disappeared from view, the old woman and the girl turned to face Floofenshire.

"Get her, Vivien," Le Fay commanded.

The little girl raised her right hand, pointing it at Lady Floofenshire. Tiny, blue bolts of lightning sparked across her arm as a ball of energy formed in her palm. Lady Floofenshire had no time to call Stevens. A blue blast enveloped her and, in an instant, she was covered in ice, her confused expression frozen on her face.

Le Fay surveyed the parlor and spied the dusty sword lying across the armchair. She licked her crusty lips. Her knees quaking, she crept across the parlor and grabbed the hilt. Percy the pelican squawked and hopped to the floor, waddling away from the strange intruder.

Blowing the dust off the blade, Morgana flipped the sword upward and admired her own reflection in the shimmering steel. Memories of her accursed brother Arthur flooded her mind. This was indeed his sword: Excalibur, the bane of evil.

Placing her other hand on the hilt and gripping ever-harder, Morgana stared at the ancient longsword and focused. Tiny wisps of green energy sprung from her fingertips, crawling up the blade and shrouding the ancient sword in a green mist.

"Hang on tight, little dears. The sword is ours, but we'll need to make a few...alterations...to Lady Floofenshire's decor to find the treasure we truly seek."

Le Fay flipped the sword blade-down and knelt, plunging the blade into floorboards. Percy ran in circles, panicked, as the house began to quake. The floorboards and walls grew cold, dark, and hard as the drywall and wood that had made up the parlor morphed into dark stone. The house's glass windows narrowed, becoming long, thin openings, and the mansion rose. A hearth burned where Lady Floofenshire's coffee table once stood.

The sorceress glided to the window, surveying the shocked crowds that had gathered around the base of her new fortress. For a moment, she considered conquering them here and now. But she contented herself with waiting. After all, there was no sense rousing the ire of the military until she was truly invincible.

There was one more spell to cast before the Black Knight and his companions arrived. Still grinning, Le Fay turned to face the horrified pelican.

As the three adventurers rounded the corner into Kensington, Bob realized it wouldn't take them long to locate Lady Floofenshire's mansion. It was, he guessed, the black, stone building that resembled a medieval fortress. Bob's stomach turned as Jeeves deactivated the rectum rocket and touched down, galloping through a throng of onlookers to Floofenshire's estate.

A deafening caw made Jeeves halt. Wind rushed by the cyber-llama as the sound of leather wings filled the air. From behind the mansion rose a scaly, purple creature the size of a house. Its eyes were red and bloodshot, and its long, scaled wings tore through the air. The monster bore a gigantic beak with a thick, wobbly pouch hanging beneath it. Opening its mouth, the beast let fly a gout of fire, scattering the screaming crowds.

The creature crashed down in front of Bob, lowering its wings and stalking the mounted adventurer. Bob drew his shield and unsheathed his sword.

"What is that thing?!" he shouted.

"Unless my zoological sensors are mistaken, sir, that's a rather large, fire-breathing pelican."

"But how can--"

"It's magic, sir. Over the years, I've found it best not to question the meddling ways of spellcasters. How do you think I got that Eleanor Roosevelt-shaped boil on my left buttock?"

Bob didn't have time to ponder his friend's anatomy. The pelican opened its beak once again, and a bolt of flame shot toward them. Jeeves galloped, dodging the fire and circling around to the back of the beast. Poised behind the monster, Jeeves bent his knees, using his pneumatic hooves to spring into the air. Bob readied his sword.

The pelican spun around, raising a wing and swatted its enemies out of the air. Like a spinning drill bit, Jeeves whirled through the air, hitting the ground and sending his master flying across the asphalt. Bob hopped up, frowning as he readied himself for the pelican.

"What was that, Jeeves?"

"You'll have to forgive me, sir. I lost my gyroscopic modulator back at the casino, and I'm afraid I'm a bit out of sorts. It'll take me a moment to regain my bearings."

"We don't have 'a moment'!"

With a mighty flap, the pelican flew, glaring at Bob and his llama. A fire blast shot toward the pair, and Bob braced himself. To his amazement, the stream of flame forked before reaching he and Jeeves. A suit of black armor appeared, and Bob saw Pellinore kneeling in front of them, using his shield to block the fire.

The fire stopped streaming from the monster's beak, and the Black Knight stood. "The beast hath focused on me now. 'Tis a good time for you to catch it unawares."

Bob nodded and crept around the Black Knight, toward the back of the creature. Noticing the pelican's shiny, purple scales, he looked at his own sword. Bob was no blacksmith, but he guessed his blade was no match for the behemoth's natural armor. He spotted the bird's legs, stowed his shield, and dove, thinking he'd slice off one of the monster's legs.

With all the strength he could muster, Bob slashed at the bird's leg. The pelican squawked, but didn't seem to be in pain. It flapped its wings once again and began to lift off the ground.

Without thinking, Bob clutched onto the fowl's leg. The pelican flapped a few more times, and Bob found himself airborne.

The creature raised its leg closer to its beak and, like a dog scratching an itch, pecked at the young adventurer. His legs awkwardly straddling the beast's right talon, Bob reached for the scales on the beast's body, cursing as his hands slipped from the smooth, purple handholds. The monster's beak scraped through his shirt, and he felt the cold, hard bill pierce his delicate skin, though he didn't feel much pain. Bob chalked it up to adrenaline and dug his sword in-between two scales.

Using the sword handle as a grip and hoisting himself closer to the creature's back, the pelican snapped at his back again. The armored bird's beak became lodged in-between Bob's shirt and his backpack, and the pelican sliced the straps, fraying the material and sliding the pack off Bob's shoulders and arms. The backpack fell toward the earth.

The scales he had clung to shot downward and Bob's sword slipped out from in-between them as the pelican dove after the backpack. Bob scrambled to grab onto the scales of the plunging bird, but they slipped through his sweaty fingers. Soon, the creature was out of reach and Bob was stranded in the air without a flying mount.

With a snap, the monstrous bird latched onto the backpack. The pelican seemed to have lost interest in Bob, content with the backpack in its beak. Yelping, Bob dropped like a pumpkin from a fifth story balcony, his eyes tearing from the wind rushing past and focused on the painful asphalt below.

"Rise, steed! Thine master is in peril!"

Jeeves staggered to his hooves. The world spun as the llama tried to orient himself without the gyroscopic modulator. Though he was unable to see his master clearly, he knew the Black Knight was right: Bob was plummeting toward the ground with no way to right himself.

"I'm afraid my flying capabilities are a bit dodgy at the moment," he said, "I'll have to deploy the airbags."

The airbag cannon popped from Jeeves' back as the llama examined Bob's descent and tried to guess the spot of earth where he would hit. Everything went fuzzy, and Jeeves' saw multiple images of his master and of the ground. He shook his head; judging exact distances was impossible in his condition.

For the first time in decades, sweat appeared on the llama's furry forehead. He'd have to solve this problem without letting his master touch the ground. Adjusting his targeting system, Jeeves aimed a little below Bob, grit hit teeth, and fired.

A square, parachute-looking capsule shot toward Bob. Jeeves nodded his head repeatedly, silently counting down to the capsule's deployment. Just as he reached zero, the airbag capsule arrived just below Bob's delicate hindquarters.

Bob caught a glimpse of the capsule as it zipped toward him. With only a fraction of a second to think, he angled his body toward the airborne pelican monster. A loud pop sounded, and the airbag blasted open. The airbag glanced his buttocks, and the force of the blast stopped his descent and shot Bob toward the sinister bird.

The pelican gripped Bob's backpack in its beak and had its wings outstretched as it made a wide turn toward the stone mansion. Bob tightened his sweaty grip on the broadsword. He was headed for the flabby, lower part of the beak.

He plunged into the spongy beak like a gumball dropped onto an angel food cake. The bird's head wobbled in all directions as it tried to shake off the intruder. But it didn't howl. The beast was desperate to hold onto Bob's backpack and clenched it in its beak ever-tighter.

Digging his free arm and legs into the squishy beak, Bob climbed. The shaking of the pelican's head made Bob feel like he was climbing a spinning ladder, but he continued his journey until the backpack was just above him.

Lifting his legs, Bob jammed his feet into the flabby bird flesh until he felt the segments of beak beneath his feet touch one another. This way, he could securely hang onto the pelican with only his feet. He'd need both hands for this.

Positioning his sword beneath the remaining backpack straps, Bob slid the sword across the canvas straps, slicing through them and causing the backpack to fall from the enemy's beak and into his free hand. Glancing over his shoulder, Bob flung the backpack straight at the Black Knight below him.

The pelican's roar blared throughout Kensington as the bird drew its wings into its body and made a dive for the falling cloth package. Bob clenched the rubbery beak as his stomach turned and the bird picked up speed. He closed his eyes to shield them from the wind and said a silent prayer; Bob hadn't been able to discuss his plan with Pellinore and had to rely on the Black Knight's combat instincts.

The armored figure had been observing the battle and, as the giant bird streamed toward him, scrambled for his sword. The Black Knight took a defensive position, digging in his heels and readying himself for whatever the young adventurer had in mind.

The bird seemed to grow more angry by the second as the backpack hit the ground just behind Pellinore. That was it! The Black Knight grabbed what remained of the backpack straps and hefted the green fabric container into the air

Opening its beak like a snake about to consume its prey, the bird plunged into the ground, taking the Black Knight with it. Bob hopped off the bird and rolled onto the pavement as the bird's head slammed into the asphalt, crushing it like a mallet hitting a fresh bagel. Then, with a muffled shriek, the bird stopped. The beast's body collapsed, falling with a clatter.

From beneath the bird's flappy lower beak crawled Pellinore, gulping down air. He placed his hands on his knees to catch his breath.

"'Twas well done, sir knight. I dost wondered whether anything other than the beast's own momentum would be enough to knock it unconscious.

The Black Knight tossed the backpack to Bob, and he examined it with a look of confusion. "Why was that thing after my backpack? It could have killed me when I was hanging onto its leg, but once it grabbed the backpack, it just lost ignored me."

"I hate to interrupt your musings, sir, rare though they are," Jeeves said, "But we may want to assess the value of your backpack on-the-go. We have, as you young folks say, bigger fish to fry."

Bob nodded and hefted the strapless backpack over his shoulder. He knew better than to ask if they should try to sneak into the castle; Le Fay had no doubt already seen their battle with the pelican. With his usual, causal gait, Jeeves trotted up to the mansion's front door and spun around, kicking it off its hinges with his hind legs. The threesome raced inside, weapons at the ready.

Chapter 7

The stone walls of the mansion blocked out the sun almost entirely. A red carpet lined the walkway, and Lady Floofenshire's parlor, once bright and lively, was now a round, stone room covered win tapestries depicting Morgana in her younger days. The mansion was filled with silence.

With Bob at their head, the three warriors crept into the cold, stone house. As he explored the parlor, Bob spotted a curious object in the corner. Tiptoeing to the object, he caught a glance of it and almost dropped his sword.

It was Lady Floofenshire frozen in a block of ice with a confused expression on her face. The cold mist of the human statue brushed against Bob's arms ,and he choked a little. Maybe he was a little too eager to face Morgana le Fay.

An orange light streamed from behind Bob and illuminated the room, casting the adventurer's shadow over the frozen woman. To Bob's rear was a stairway leading further into the mansion. A girl and boy like the ones that had accompanied le Fay into the casino stood atop the staircase.

The girl held her hand palm-up and an orange energy ball hovered above it. The boy stretched out his arms and held out his hands, as if waiting to receive something. With a zotting sound, the ball of mystic power dissolved into wisps of orange light and, like glowing tadpoles, weaved around the boy.

A breastplate, pauldrons, a horned helmet, and gauntlets formed around the little tyke. Soon, he was wearing a full suit of armor and wielding a claymore sword almost twice his size. The boy hopped onto the marble banister and slid toward his quarry, the armor scraping the railing as he made his way to the parlor.

The boy leapt off the banister and landed before the Black Knight. Staring straight into the eye slits of the ancient warrior's

119

helmet, the boy planted his sword into the ground. He continued to look at Pellinore, as if expecting him to speak.

At first, the Black Knight said nothing. But soon his arms drooped and he took a step back.

"You....," he muttered, "It's you. But, how did you...that's impossible."

The boy grinned. It was the first time Bob had seen one of these children smile, and he really wished he hadn't. Raising his huge sword, the boy swung at Pellinore. Caught off-guard, the Black Knight barely had time to raise his shield and block the strike. Staggering, he struck at the child with his own blade, but the boy dodged.

The young girl descended the stairs gracefully, her hands at her sides and her fingers outstretched like claws. As she reached the bottom of the stairs, she glared at Bob and Jeeves. Sparks of purple energy crackled around her fingertips, and she planted herself between the adventurers and the front door.

Jeeves nodded at his master. "Go ahead and brandish your weapon, sir. It's only a little girl."

"Thanks, Jeeves."

Turning the broadsword so he'd strike with the flat of the blade, Bob ran toward the girl. She raised her palm, and a purple energy blast shot at Bob. He positioned his shield in front of the blast, and his knees buckled as the mystic burst of power made his knees buckle.

A fine powder poured across Bob's arm. Bob pried his eyes open and found himself holding a shield handle attached to nothing as a pile of ash trickled from his forearm to the floor. The blast had dissolved his shield!

Bob dove to the left and rolled as another purple blast hit the stone floor. Like a hunted rabbit, Bob dodged from one corner of the parlor to another, twisting as he tried to avoid the little girl's bursts of magic energy.

The boy hit the Black Knight with a barrage of strikes on his shield and breastplate. The claymore's weight didn't slow the tyke down, but Pellinore seemed unaffected by the dents in his armor. Shoving his shield-arm forward, he made his enemy jump backward.

"Take that, cur!" Pellinore shouted as a sword-strike to the side of the helmet sent the sinister child to the floor, "Thy presence makes my heart near burst with rage. But I suppose I must thank thee; Today, I shalt not only complete another noble quest, but attain vengeance for all Camelot!"

The boy simply chuckled, stood, and rested the giant sword on his shoulder, motioning for the Black Knight to attack. Pellinore charged down the hallway like an angry bull. He struck at his opponent's legs, but the child hopped out of the way.

The Black Knight raised his shield as the giant sword craned toward his skull. Ramming his shoulder into the child warrior, Pellinore continued his charge and smashed through the kitchen door. Wood splinters scattered as the two slammed into the kitchen table.

The child raised his foot and placed it on the Black Knight's breastplate. With a mighty shove, the short knight kicked his opponent away. Each combatant landed on his feet, standing on either side of the oak kitchen table.

The tapestry he hid behind exploded into ash, and Bob sprinted behind the next. He was running out of places to hide. Bob smacked his dry tongue against the roof of his mouth as he watched the ash swirl around him and thought of his own delicate flesh.

As he faced the little girl once again, Bob's mind clicked into place and he forgot his fear. Each time she fired a blast, she used only her left hand. Dodging another magic beam, Bob hopped onto his llama.

"Sir," Jeeves stammered as the girl raised her glowing palm toward him, "Do you mind telling me what in the name of Roy Rogers you think you're doing?"

"The bubble gum cannon, Jeeves!"

Spreading his four legs and making his knees rigid, Jeeves produced the sleek gun from his midsection and fired two sticky blasts. The first hit the girl's attack in midair, turning the bubble gum to ash. The other wad of gum smacked the girl's left hand, enveloping her hand in a blob of pink goo.

The child grimaced. Tension built in her hand and she shook a little as a bubble in the gum wad took shape. With a squish, it popped and then deflated like a sad, sad balloon.

"Good show, sir. But I'm afraid I may have neglected my duties as your guide."

"What do you mean?"

"Well sir, as you've been the primary target of both the pelican and this young lady due to that dreadful sack of useless junk you've been dragging around, it occurs to me that one of us ought to confront le Fay herself with the backpack in tow."

"'One of us' ought to. You're not talking about yourself, are you?"

"No, sir. Le Fay was clearly not content with snatching Excalibur from Lady Floofenshire and instead wishes to obtain your backpack. Because she's insane and delusional, I suppose. Off you go, then."

Jumping onto his front legs and thrusting his derriere up, Jeeves catapulted his master over the girl's head and toward the stone stairway the two children had strode down moments ago.

The girl whirled around, blue energy swirling around her free hand as she prepared to freeze her quarry. But a terse farting sound told her the llama's rectal propulsion system had been activated. Jeeves landed in front of the girl, shielding Bob.

"Godspeed, sir," the llama said, twisting his monocle and fixing his gaze on the child.

Bob nodded and scrambled up the stairs.

The girl's eyes narrowed, and she seethed at the well-dressed llama. Jeeves planted his front hoof in her face, as if disciplining her.

"My young friend and I have had quite enough of your behavior, young lady. The black arts are nothing to be trifled with. I should know. I used to dabble in mysticism myself. And let's just say the hippo from the local zoo won't be returning from the dark dimension any time soon."

The girl shot a freeze blast at the annoying creature, which he sidestepped as the metal panels on his sides slid aside, revealing the familiar bean bag cannons. She completed a series of hand motions and a glowing, green circle covered in runes appeared on her right arm.

Thrusting her arm up and then down, the little girl deflected every bean bag as through she were wielding a shield. Each bag hit the ground with a soft thud. As she traipsed around the room, Jeeves rotated, keeping his rate of fire steady.

Dropping beneath the stream of bean bag fire, the youngster pointed her fist toward the llama. The glowing disc flew at the furry creature with the speed of a greased cheetah. Jeeves leaned to his left, cursing as the disc sliced through one of his bean bag cannons and continued on its path, cutting through the house's stone wall.

"You'll need to do better than that, my dear. I've had plenty of experience twisting and turning my body. Believe it or not, I was rather skilled on the dance floor in my day."

It was clear to Jeeves what he had to do. Each of the child's spells was coming from her right hand now, and without the use of her palms, she was powerless. But the girl had learned from the bubble gum cannon incident; she had no intention of letting the quadruped get close enough to fire the gooey weapon.

Kneeling, the girl placed her palm on the ground. Like a spark through gunpowder, a red line of energy snaked across the ground, drawing a glowing circle around the llama. Grinning, she ignited the fire.

A burst of flame shot from the floor, catching Jeeves off-guard. He yelped and ignited his own rocket as the fire scalded his tushie. Rising just above the flames, Jeeves snorted.

"Well, you ghastly little thingg, now you've made me angry."

Jeeves opened his mouth much wider than he ever had before. And it kept opening. The maw of the llama grew more and more vast as though he were a snake preparing to swallow its prey. The girl prepared a freezing spell, and her right arm glowed with a familiar blue energy.

A moist cantaloupe shot from Jeeves mouth, walloping the nasty child in the face. She dropped to the stone floor and lay motionless. The tower of fire vanished, and Jeeves deactivated the rectum rocket.

Trotting to the child, Jeeves prepared the bubble gum cannon and focused on her right hand, which still surged with the blue magic. Jeeves snickered as he took aim.

The little girl popped up, thrusting her hand in the llama's face. A frosty blast enveloped the quadruped and, like Lady Floofenshire, Jeeves became a frozen statue.

Nodding at her handiwork, the girl turned her attention to the sounds of battle in the kitchen. Her comrade was still locked in battle with the Black Knight. That, she thought, would soon change. A white glow enveloped her hand as she strode toward the kitchen.

A thunderous smash of ice echoed through the castle halls as a metal tentacle snaked from frozen llama and snapped onto the young mage's ankle, flipping her upside down and lifting her.

Before she could reorient herself, a pink glob of gum smacked into her right hand, encasing it completely. She was facing the frigid creature now and watched with eyebrows raised as metal panels shifted open and closed as tiny ice sheets cracked and shattered. Once he was fully mobile, Jeeves retracted his arm, bringing the little whelp face-to-face.

"A clever move, my friend," Jeeves chortled, ice particles still clinging to his fur, "Very clever indeed. But unlike our dear Lady Floofenshire, I don't have a human circulatory system. A little cold isn't much of a deterrent when one possesses a thermo-nuclear energy core."

The boy blocked strike after strike as the enraged Black Knight hacked at his opponent, barely missing the kitchen table. Sidestepping, the kid swung his sword to the side, smacking the sable warrior's shield with all his strength.

Grunting, the phantom dropped to one knee. His opponent was even stronger now than he had been years ago. But Sir Pellinore was determined. His breath grew heavy as he thought of endless nights around the hearth trading tales of adventuring with his fellow knights. It was time, at last, to end this conflict and avenge every one of his friends.

"For Perceval!" he shouted, springing with his blade upraised. The child leaned backward.

Bashing his opponent in the breastplate, the Black Knight sent the lad staggering closer to the end of the table. "For Lancelot!"

The child fell on his bottom as the specter's blade came crashing down on his helmet. "For Arthur!"

Rolling onto his back, the boy thrust his leg up, kicking the Black Knight in the chin. Sir Pellinore fell onto his back plates. Teetering on the edge of the table, the armor child staggered to his feet. He placed the tip of his sword at the Black Knight's throat.

"For me," he growled in a deep baritone.

Pellinore shifted his arms, placing his palms flat against the table on either side of his head. "For Camelot."

The Black Knight hoisted himself up, and the boy's claymore clinked against the knight's breastplate and away from his neck. Pellinore flew backward, twisting his body into a backflip, and brought his feet down on the other end of the table.

The head of the wooden table flew up like the end of a see saw, and the child was thrust into the stone ceiling. The horns of his helmet rammed into the rock, leaving the boy lodged in the stone. The Black Knight swatted his wrist, causing the tiny warrior to drop his blade.

Pellinore drew his arm back, his sword raised. "At last. My friends, my king, every soul in the land—every one shall be avenged."

With a clank, something grabbed onto the tip of the Black Knight's sword. He whipped around to see the cyber-llama, covered in frost but otherwise unharmed, gripping the blade with its metallic tentacle.

"What treachery is this?!" the ancient knight cried, "Release my blade! Camelot must be avenged!"

"You're not the only one here who's oathbound, my Fun Onion-munching friend. This enemy has been defeated once again and won't be able to menace England anymore. Can you content yourself with that?"

The Black Knight lowered his blade and sighed. "Thou art wise, llama. I shalt not soil my sword with the blood of a child."

He turned to face the child embedded in the ceiling, "But mark mine words, traitor: if thou shouldst menace this land again, I will find thee. And I will stop thee. Time and time again."

The sounds of Jeeves' battle in the parlor had dissolved completely. The stone steps leading to the upper floor of the fortress went on longer than Bob had expected. They led to a hallway, and Bob tiptoed across it, expecting to see an old lady pop out of every corner. At the end of the stone hall was another staircase; this one spiraled upward. He shuddered as he passed the many rooms of the mansion. Each, he imagined, had once held Lady Floofenshire's possessions.

Now, each room featured a different tapestry depicting a young le Fay performing some act of deceit. One bore the inscription "Morgana le Fay convinces Merlin to leave Arthur's side", another "Morgana le Fay leads eighteen knights to their deaths on the Isle of Avalon", and still another "Morgana le Fay eats the last chocolate pudding cup, leaving the king with only vanilla."

Drawing closer to the spiral stairs, Bob heard the faint swish of metal; Le Fay practicing with Excalibur, no doubt. Just before he began to climb the stairs, Bob spotted another tapestry.

This one was blank, just a dark red square of fabric. The young adventurer creeped closer to the new decoration, looking behind him every few seconds to make the enchantress didn't take him by surprise.

The empty tapestry, like the others, contained an inscription at the bottom: "Morgana le Fay slays Bob Halibut just after recovering the sword Excalibur."

Bob cleared his throat as he noticed for the first time how cold the stone mansion was. Flopping the strapless backpack over his shoulder once again, he shuffled toward the stairs and climbed them to the third floor.

He climbed the final stair and stepped into what had been Lady Floofenshire's bedroom. Torchlight cast shadows into every corner, and a series of shields with crossed swords hung across the walls. Two long tables stood on the northern and southern sides of the room, each adorned with golden goblets and silverware made of real silver.

At one end of the room stood the old woman, running her fingers across the ancient sword like a greedy child. The corners of her wrinkled lips were curled up in a smile as a green mist swirled around the blade.

"How do you like my new throne room, dearie?" le Fay asked, keeping her eyes on Excalibur, "I've just finished setting up the decorations and dining arrangements. All that's left to construct is a throne. I was rather hoping for a nice llama-skin chair. What do you think?"

Bob drew his broadsword, his eyes darting around the room and searching for traps. "Why do you want my backpack?"

Le Fay lifted her head and cocked an eyebrow. "Because Floofenshire's estate is just the beginning. That green, canvas bag holds the key to establishing my kingdom over all Britannia. You wouldn't begrudge a poor, old lady that, would you?"

Bob shifted his left hand's grip on the backpack, securing it over his shoulder as best he could.

The medieval enchantress shrugged. "So be it." Placing her other gnarled hand on the mystic sword's handle, she charged at Bob, the sinister grin still on her face.

Chapter 8

The ancient sword smashed against Bob's own blade, and the impact made him falter. He tried to strike at le Fay's side, but the old lady parried his sword and struck twice herself, slicing Bob just above the ear. Pain shot though the side of his face. He expected to feel cold blood trickle down to his earlobe, but sensed nothing.

"You remind me of my brother," Morgana cried, swatting at Bob's head with a hacking motion, "Always the kingly champion of light and justice and all that rubbish. Always blind to the power that lies at your fingertips."

Bob deflected the sorceress' attacks and realized she was forcing him toward the stairway. Bob planted his feet, and his blade shot toward le Fay's head. She ducked, punching Bob in the stomach.

Dropping to the floor in pain, Bob rolled, avoiding the point of Excalibur as Morgana plunged it into the throne room's floor. Bob righted himself, running at his opponent once again.

"I don't know what you're talking about, wrinkly wench," Bob said, amazed by his deep tone of voice, "but since I've been given the chance to stand between you and innocent people, I have a duty to make sure you never leave this house."

Bob stabbed, trying to strike le Fay. She deflected his strike and tried to hit him in the side once again, crossing blades.

They sidestepped across the tower, exchanging blows one after another, until both heaved with exhaustion. As Bob's sword smacked against Excalibur for the fiftieth time, Morgana hopped away, lowering the blade.

"I'm getting tired of this," she huffed, "You're a more talented swordfighter than I'd first guessed. But blades were never my specialty, anyway."

She extended the sword in Bob's direction. The green mist that had surrounded Excalibur gathered together, forming a swirling beam that shot toward Bob. He dove against the floor.

A ball of fire appeared in the sorceress' free hand. She lobbed the flame at Bob and he leapt to the side, the fire singeing the edges of his jeans. Another blast of green mist from Excalibur whizzed past him. He had to find a way to get back into sword range.

The maniacal old woman continued to lob fireballs at him and. As Bob hopped around the pools of flame, he noticed that the additional light allowed him to see the room's decorations more clearly. Sheathing his sword, Bob grabbed his laser pistol and took aim at one of the shields hanging on the wall just above his head. A laser blast dislodged the round shield.

He holstered his pistol and caught the shield. Flinging it across the room, he heard a thud and a groan as the buckler smacked le Fay in the face. Bob dashed toward his foe and pulled out his sword once again, swinging at Morgana's neck.

The old woman parried the ancient broadsword just before it reached her. Her smile was long gone. Surging forward, she wrapped her arms around Bob's shoulders, wrapping him in the strangest hug he'd ever been a part of.

Placing Excalibur between Bob's back and his backpack, Morgana sliced upward. The backpack ripped open, spilling its contents just behind Bob. A coil of rope, a large compass, several pencils, a first aid kit, a few granola bars, Excalibur's scabbard, and a book on tape entitled *Trixx are for Kids: One Rabbit's Battle with Species-Based Discrimination* scattered across the stone floor.

Le Fay released Bob and bolted behind him, dropping to her knees. Magic trinkets and pouches fell out of her pockets as she snatched the scabbard. Her hands trembled and she rose, looking like a child who'd just found out where his parents had hidden the Christmas presents.

While his opponent was distracted, Bob surveyed the area around his backpack. He grabbed a curious pouch, which he stuffed into his pocket, and raised his sword, ready for Morgana's next attack.

"At last," le Fay muttered, drooling a bit, "At last the scabbard of Excalibur is mine. Now, dear brother, I am truly invincible."

She shoved the bejeweled scabbard into her belt and faced the confused adventurer, Excalibur in her hands once again. "The true treasure of Arthur was never his sword, young Halibut. After he battled your friend the Black Knight and obtained Excalibur, the wizard Merlin told my goody-two-shoes brother of the true power he possessed. The one who wields Excalibur's sheath cannot be wounded; no blade, bullet, or other weapon can pierce their flesh."

Morgana advanced on Bob like a poodle on a steak. "Once I've slain thee, Halibut, I'll conquer all of this miserable land and the reign of Queen Morgana the Invulnerable shall commence. And between the scabbard and the anti-aging spells, I should be able to make my kingdom last a good few eras."

Another green blast erupted from Excalibur. Caught by surprise, Bob flew back and smacked into the black stone, a sharp pain shooting up his back. He leapt to his feet, preparing for le Fay's next attack.

Bearing her corn-like teeth, the ancient lady surged toward Bob, swinging Excalibur like a one-eyed kid swinging at a tee ball. Winding his own sword in every direction to block le Fay's strikes, Bob's mind raced as he searched for the perfect opportunity. If he didn't choose the right moment to spring his trap, he'd find himself without a head.

Stretching her arms behind her head and down her back, Morgana prepared for a mighty cleave. She brought the sword down on her opponent like a sledgehammer on a railroad spike. Bob raised his own blade to deflect it.

With a booming smash, the Black Knight's broadsword shattered before Excalibur. Metal shards and splinters sprawled across the stone bricks and Bob fell, thwacking into the ground once again. He grew pale as he stared at the hilt and sword fragment in his fist.

Le Fay threw her head back and laughed like a teenage girl who'd overdosed on nitrous oxide. "Didn't Pellinore tell you of his battle with my brother, boy? His old sword was no match for Excalibur, and neither is that one."

As Morgana monologued, Bob reached into his pocket and pulled the string of the pouch he'd grabbed from the castle floor, pouring a handful of powder into his palm.

"You'll be seeing both of them in a minute. You can ask them yourself!"

Le Fay swung the sword toward the middle of Bob's head, ready to cleave him in twain. When Excalibur's blade was inches from his forehead, Bob raised his hand and blew a handful of powder in Morgana's face.

The ancient blade froze, just a hair away from Bob's delicate cranium. Crab-walking away from Morgana, Bob bounded to his feet and stood face-to-face with the conjurer. She was still as a statue; the whites of her eyes had turned a solid orange.

"Give me the sword and the scabbard," Bob told the sorceress

Like a dog bringing slippers to its master, le Fay yanked the scabbard from her belt and held it and Excalibur in her outstretched hands. Bob stowed the sheath in his own belt and gripped the legendary sword. He pushed the air out of his cheeks, relieved.

It was a good thing le Fay had labeled her magic powders with easy-to-read graphics. Without the "brain-encircled-by-hands" rune, he never would have guessed the pouch he'd snagged contained mind-control powder.

For a moment, he considered what to do with the evil sorceress. Now that she wasn't throwing fireballs at him, Bob noticed the toll the years had taken on her.

Her wrinkled flesh and gray, yarn-like hair bore little resemblance to the young woman he'd seen on the tapestries that lined the hallway. Perhaps, after living in the shadow of her kingly brother for centuries, it was time someone showed Morgana le Fay sympathy and gave her a chance to repent of her evil ways and do good.

He shook his head. Now was no time for sympathy. Not for one this evil.

Bob cleared his throat "Banish yourself," he commanded, "Use your mystic arts to banish yourself to some distant dimension."

Le Fay nodded. With one wave or her hands, she disappeared in a burst of magic energy.

The helmet was barely recognizable and only one of the horns remained, but the child had managed to free himself from the kitchen ceiling after his battle with Pellinore. The American and his llama and the ghost were gone now. His dented armor clanking awkwardly, the child dashed up the stairs.

Reaching the top of the spiral staircase, the boy froze. Morgana was gone.

The little boy cast his helmet aside and ran to the nearby bedroom mirror. As he suspected, he could see her visage in the mirror. She'd been banished!

"Mother," the boy said in a deep, raspy voice.

"Curse that Halibut and his llama!" Morgana spat, looking back through the mirror, "There's no escape from this dimension!"

"What can I do, mother?"

"Avenge me, Lil' Mordred. Seize your birthright and make Halibut and his llama pay for the indignities they've inflicted on our family."

The young boy curled his armored fingers into a fist, gritting his teeth and lusting for llama blood.

Bob felt a little apprehensive as he and the cyber-llama trudged along the forest path toward the mystical lake. He stared at Excalibur and its scabbard. The morning sun flickered off each gem in the hilt, creating a rainbow of light that glistened off the edge of the lake.

Why, he thought, shouldn't he just take the sword and scabbard back to Grandma Edwina's mansion? It'd be safer there, and a scabbard that made him immune to all wounds would make adventuring a breeze.

"I know what you're thinking, sir," Jeeves piped up, "and the answer is no. The Lady of the Lake is Excalibur's rightful owner."

Bob nodded and knelt, tapping the edge of the lake with the edge of the scabbard as he'd done before. There was a rustle beneath the water as the Lady appeared, sauntering across the water gracefully.

The Lady smiled and looked down at the elaborate weapon and sheath in Bob's hands.

"Well met, young warrior," she said, "Thou hast found mine toilet plunger. I had thought I should never see the swirling waters of mine toilet again. You have my eternal gratitude."

Bob nodded and presented the sword to the Lady. She lay it across her palms, sinking beneath the water's surface, back to her watery home. Bob and Jeeves watched as she and even for a few minutes after she disappeared.

"Are you going to return to your castle right away, Sir Pellinore?" Bob asked.

There was no answer.

"I said, are you going to return to you—"

"He's gone, sir. The Black Knight fulfilled his mission."

"Does that mean he's gone for good?"

146

"I'm the wrong llama to ask about the paranormal, sir. Ghosts are as much a mystery to me as they are to you. But I expect that, if his native isle falls into peril again, the Black Knight won't stand idly by. He's a knight of the Round Table, after all."

As the sun set over the surface of the lake, Bob squinted. Something was caught in the breeze, blowing toward him like a falling leaf. Gradually, the flat object floated into view. At last, the empty bag of Cheesy Chips (for that's what it was) landed in Bob's hand, sprinkling his fingers with orange dust. Bob chuckled. Adventurers, he realized, never really die.